Versipellis
Lupus
Venandi

By
C.J. Laurence

To Andie,

Thank you for buying!
Hope you enjoy it ☺

C.Laurence xx

Versipellis Lupus Venandi

READER INFORMATION

You will consistently notice the spelling of the word 'magic' as 'magick' throughout this series. This IS intentional and NOT a spelling mistake.

Some of you may already be aware of the difference between the two, but for those of you who aren't, here is a brief overview to give you a better idea:

Magic is something attributed to magicians. The likes of Paul Daniels, Harry Houdini, David Blaine, David Copperfield, Derren Brown, Dynamo…

Basically, those who are skilled in the fine art of optical illusions.

Magick is something attributed most famously to Aleister Crowley. Those of you who are familiar with his name will no doubt already know his famous quote – *'Magick is the Science and Art of causing Change to occur in conformity with Will.'*

In essence, the addition of the letter 'k' distinguishes spiritual discipline from stage magic and sleight of hand tricks.

Where it concerns my characters, and the forthcoming tale, it is used from the perspective of magical realism, hence using the alternative spelling.

Versipellis Lupus Venandi

Cover Designer: Methyss Digital Art

Dedication
To all of you who believe in the supernatural—
this is for you.

1
Beginnings
Katana—her fifth birthday

Most little girls at the tender age of five are dreaming of unicorns, Hello Kitty, and anything pink and glittery.

But Katana Kempe was not like most little girls. It wasn't that she was deformed in some way or even had a genius level IQ, but it was more the fact that her family hunted werewolves for a living. To them, werewolves were as normal in their lives as dogs in the lives of humans.

However, the truth of the existence of werewolves was still very much a shrouded secret. Stories had banded about the world for centuries of men turning into rabid, blood-thirsty creatures, but only ever on a full-moon.

In the UK, the threat of werewolves had been ever present to the extent that by the seventeenth century, official records stated that not even natural wolves were in existence anymore. All traces of wolves, natural and supernatural, were long gone from the country.

To Katana Kempe, her bedtime stories to blissfully lull her into a deep sleep were not of princes and princesses finding their happily ever after, but of monstrous creatures rising from the darkness, horrid abominations of nature that her family slayed to keep people safe.

She'd heard the story hundreds of times—the tale of Henry Kempe, her infamous ancestor who started this journey for the Kempe family.

"His courage in the face of danger is still unrivalled to this day," Malaceia, Katana's father said, settling her into bed. "He knew their town was being stalked by a rabid beast. He knew whatever it was happened to be so grotesque and such a freak of nature that only he could take it on. When a third little girl went missing from her bed, Henry knew he had to take action."

Katana's bright blue eyes grew wide with fear. "A little girl went missing from her bed? Just like me?"

Malaceia nodded. "She was older than you, but yes, she was just like you. But you are so much safer. Death himself couldn't break in here without someone knowing about it and coming to protect you."

Katana gave her daddy a big grin and snuggled down under her plain blue duvet, ready for the rest of the story.

"Henry tried telling his towns folk of what he had seen but he was laughed at. So, he took his dog and mounted his horse and rode off into the forest. He returned six days later dragging the body of a beastly wolf and carrying its head on a stick. The kill was so fresh, its blood was still drying on his white riding cape. In fact, there had been so much blood spilled, his white riding hood was now painted red—red with the blood of his kill. That's how we got our name, petal— The Red Riding Hoods."

"I wish I could meet Henry," Katana whispered, snuffling into her warm bedclothes. "He'd have been so big and so strong."

Malaceia nodded. "He was, petal. He was an incredible man. When the towns folk saw what he was carrying into the square, gasps and screams sounded around him. Before their very eyes, the headless body withered back into that of a man. When someone fetched the good King himself, it was decided there and then that Henry Kempe would now be revered as the expert in ridding the land of such wicked creatures."

Katana clapped her hands together and squealed, her eyes gleaming with excitement. "Daddy, tell the rest!"

"Henry had caught the beast feasting on the girl's heart, liver, and kidneys. He knew this must mean something to them as nothing else on her delicate body had been harmed. So, in front of the town, in the middle of the square, he gutted the man's body and removed the same three organs. Then, in three separate fires, he burned the body, the organs, and the head to nothing but a pile of ashes."

"And then?"

"And then King John congratulated Henry on such a fantastic job and bestowed upon him all the weapons and money he would ever need to complete the task of killing all of these creatures throughout the whole land."

"And then he got married and had lots of children and taught them all to be just like him."

Malaceia playfully tapped the end of his daughter's button nose. "Exactly. And his children had children and taught them all the same, and it followed on through the centuries until we end up with you here, today."

"And I'm going to be just like Henry," Katana said, her small voice full of pride and conviction. "And you, Daddy."

Malaceia nodded and pulled his lips into a thin line. "But there is lots to learn first, petal. Now, it's time for sweet dreams before your first big day of training tomorrow."

After a kiss on the cheek from her beloved father, Katana drifted off into a deep sleep full of werewolves dying at her hands.

Katana—her sixteenth birthday

It was the morning of her sweet sixteen, but for Katana it was merely another day closer to being out in the field, hunting these creatures and protecting the innocent from their monstrous paws.

She hadn't even opened a card or said thank you to her parents for her presents she had yet to open; she had questions that needed answers.

Storming into her father's office, she threw the Kempe family history book that she'd been given as a child on his desk and folded her arms over her chest.

"But, how, Dad? I don't understand how Henry knew to cut all those organs out and burn them separately. It doesn't make sense. Any normal person would think that cutting the head off something would be more than enough to kill it."

Malaceia shrugged his shoulders and sighed. "I don't know, Katana. Call it gut instinct or whatever, but he just knew that's what had to be done, so he did it. It obviously worked out for the best, hmmm? You ask far too many questions instead of just accepting what *is*." Malaceia clapped his hands together. "Now, have you reconsidered Tobias Bembridge's offer?"

Katana rolled her eyes. "I'm not interested, Dad. I'm sixteen now which means I have one more year of training before I can go out into the field and start killing these things in the real world."

"But we can't let our bloodlines dry up, Katana. As a woman, you do have a right to bear children."

"No," Katana said, slapping her hand down on his mahogany desk. "I have the ability to bear children. It doesn't mean I want to."

"But the allegiances, Katana. If you married Tobias Bembridge, you'd be uniting The Red Riding Hoods with one of the greatest Preternatural Council families there are. Do you not understand how that could ensure our future?"

Katana narrowed her eyes at her father and set her hands on her hips. "Our future is dependent on werewolf numbers, not politically arranged marriages. Quit trying to marry me off already."

Malaceia sighed and scrubbed his shovel-sized hands over his face. "I wish you'd give up on this ghost of a dream of going out into the field, Katana. It's not where women belong. It's a man's world. Even for regular humans, hunting of any kind is a man's world."

Katana snorted. "And we're also in the modern age where equality is ever present amongst the genders, Dad. Why have you even bothered to train me all these years if you didn't want me to go out in the field?"

"It's a requirement that all Kempe children go through the training regime. Think of it as compulsory self-defence classes."

Katana screwed her nose up. "Are you kidding? So what, you figured that by now I'd be more interested in boys and nail varnish like all the other females in this family? Except aunt Marion of course."

Malaceia shrugged his shoulders. "Something like that, yes."

"What makes me less capable of killing a werewolf than Brogan or Ethan? Hell, they've had dozens of slip-ups in their live training sessions—I've had three."

"Exactly. Three that could have resulted in your death."

"And they had dozens that could have ended the same way."

"Your brothers are more than aware of that when they start fighting. They know the consequences of their bad decisions."

Katana lifted her hands up in front of her and waved. "Err, hello."

"No, Katana," Malaceia said. He stood behind his desk and slammed his fists down onto it. The practice of doing this over the years had begun to leave concave imprints in his antique wooden furniture. "You're a female and it's always different for the females."

"Aunt Marion did it." Katana hoped that bringing back memories of her dad's younger sister would work in her favour. "She got over three hundred kills in her lifetime."

Malaceia leaned forwards and sneered in his daughter's face. "Exactly. And where is she now? Pushing up daisies because she made one mistake. And she didn't even leave one child to carry on the bloodline."

Without even thinking, Katana slapped her father around the face. The resounding crack from her palm meeting his solid cheek shocked her into realising what she'd done. She turned and ran.

After that, she didn't even dare be in the same vicinity as her father for several weeks. She learned through her mother, though, that she'd earned herself another years' training after her seventeenth birthday.

"For discipline," her mother said. "All great hunters must follow a strict code of discipline."

"Great," she muttered. "Another two years of this crap."

"If your father hears you say that, expect another addition to your disciplinary sentence."

Too stubborn for her own good, it Katana a little while to work out that sometimes keeping her mouth shut was the best way.

Katana—two weeks after her twenty-second birthday

She crept through the forest, step by step. Moonlight highlighted the path ahead, picking out the fallen twigs and bundles of dead leaves. A faint glimmer of orange light danced a mere few hundred yards away. A gentle breeze swept over her, sending a small chill down her spine.

Nearly at Grandma's, she thought. *Nearly in the warm with delicious food and a solid roof over my head.*

Reaching the front door, she pushed it open, shouting over the creak of its hinges. "Grandma, Grandma, where are you? I've brought your favourite meatloaf."

"In the bedroom, dear," replied a croaky voice. "I'm not feeling too well."

She crossed the tiny kitchen and approached the closed bedroom door. When she opened it, there sat Grandma, in bed, wearing her dressing gown and woolly hat, and cuddling a hot water bottle to her chest.

"Oh, Grandma. You don't look well at all. What a big nose you have!"

"Dear child, all the better to smell that beautiful meatloaf with."

"Your eyes are so big, Grandma. Do you need a cool cloth?"

"No, dear. They just allow me to see your sweet innocence even better."

Katana walked around the side of her Grandma's bed and sat down next to her. Taking hold of her gran's forearm, she gasped. "Oh, Grandma! How warm and cuddly your arms are."

"All to make our hugs better, sweet child."

Katana put her hand in the basket and pulled out the meatloaf she'd so carefully wrapped earlier that afternoon. Carefully undoing the greaseproof paper, she exposed the divine smelling brown loaf that made her own stomach grumble.

"Would you like me to cut you some, Grandma? I bet it'll make you feel better."

"You spoil me, dear. That would be lovely, thank you."

Before Katana could even think, an ear ringing punch knocked her clean off the bed, sending her sprawling through the air. When her head connected with the hard-wooden wall behind her, stars danced before her eyes.

Grandma flew out of bed, ripping her nightclothes from her body. Only it wasn't Grandma beneath the clothes; it was a huge white wolf.

Standing on its back legs, it stalked towards its prey, snapping its jaws with every step. Drool dangled from its pink gums.

Katana sighed and screamed in frustration. She glanced up at the top corner of the bedroom, knowing what was up there.

Making eye contact with the small, black hole, she stuck her middle finger up at it and glared at whoever was watching.

"Are you fucking serious?" she said, climbing to her feet.

The wolf stopped in his tracks. His shoulders drooped, and he whined as he sat down on the bed. "Was it me?" he said. "Was I not scary enough? Did I hurt you?"

Katana rolled her eyes at her insecure friend. He had more social anxiety issues than a teenage girl. "I'm fine, Jacques. You were fine. It's these idiots expecting me to still be training like this and taking them seriously."

"Katana!" Malaceia shouted, storming into the cabin. "What the hell do you think you're doing? You do know these training exercises cost money, right?"

As her father strode in, bustling all of his six-foot-six height and two-hundred-pound mass of muscles, Katana dropped her defiant gaze to the floor. She'd never admit it to anyone, but angering her father was the only thing she feared. However, sometimes it was needed to make a point.

"Dad, come on. I'm twenty-two years old and you got me going over training scenarios I did when I was six. I know all of the moves this little role-play takes and I can also win every single one blindfolded."

"Pride comes before a fall, Katana. There is nothing wrong with going back to basics."

"Dad, you sent Leon out into the field when he was barely seventeen. Ethan was hunting on his seventeenth birthday. Even the others had barely passed a week of being seventeen before you packed them off hunting. Yet here I am, being treated like a baby. Hell, by the time Brogan was my age, he'd killed over a hundred werewolves already. Come on, Dad. Give me a chance."

Malaceia stared at his defiant daughter. Growing up with six older brothers had left her with little innocence or fears about broken nails.

Still, being a female in this world was not easy. Unlike her brothers, Katana had too much of her own mind for Malaceia to class her as a confident hunter. He had a duty as her father to protect her. "Sometimes it's the simple things that catch us off track."

She sighed and strolled over to the basket full of fresh meatloaf. "Let's not make this about uncle Arald. For once."

Malaceia balled his fists at the mention of his twin's name. "This isn't about Arald," he said, forcing each word through gritted teeth. "Why does everyone keep saying that? I couldn't give two shits about damn Arald!"

Seeing the hatred oozing from his face, Katana struggled not to laugh. When her father looked like this, she likened it to the evil face pulled by her first horse, Hestallia.

The chestnut mare had a unique ability to almost curdle milk with the sour, empty stare she'd give right before she whipped around and barrelled people in the face with both back feet. It had been a handy move to have in live training though—it caught many a werewolf off guard, buying Katana valuable seconds to gain the upper hand. Hestallia was now retired, and her son, Katana's current horse, Altair, was much more amenable and used his speed rather than his back feet to gain time.

Upon hearing Malaceia swear, Jacques gasped. He never swore. That fact in itself was more surprising than the fact Jacques was a talking wolf.

"Dad, we're concerned, that's all," Katana said. "It's not every day you discover your twin brother has been having an affair with your arch enemy."

Malaceia's nostrils flared to a degree a racehorse would crave for. After several silent seconds, he finally said, "Do you really think you're ready to go out in the field?"

Katana smirked and decided not to pick him up on his change of subject. "Yes, Dad. I'm more than ready."

"Fine," he said, seeming to calm down to a quiet simmer. "I guess I still see you as my little girl, that's all. I'm worried about letting you go out there on your own."

"I won't be alone, Dad. I've got Jacques."

Malaceia looked at his daughter's shaggy haired companion and snorted. "It was a metaphor, sweetie. You may as well be alone for all the use he is. I really wish you'd take Calhoun or Dylan instead. Plus, don't forget Tobias Bembridge is still asking for you. If you end up hurt or injured, he may not be interested anymore."

Exasperated for this conversation for the thousandth time, Katana sighed. "Dad, we've been over this a million times. Jacques is a skilled fighter and an intelligent match for me. Calhoun is an arrogant brute and Dylan is always more interested in chasing the nearest bitch in heat. As for Tobias, that's not even a discussion we're going to have."

Malaceia glanced over at Jacques who was now on the floor on all fours, ears drooping, tail between his legs and his belly touching the floor. "At least I know you'd be protected. Look at him, Katana. For goodness sake."

"Remember what you always taught me about the wolves? That we need to be thankful for them. Being raised by witches and learning to talk isn't the easy life some might think."

He pulled his lips into a thin line and clenched his jaw. "Yes, I remember."

"Right, so the fact he's not a wrecking ball should be embraced, and he should be allowed to utilise the skills he does have. Do you agree?"

"Yes, Katana," Malaceia sighed. "Just…not utilising them alongside you. Anyone but you." He scrubbed his hands over his face. "I should have put my foot down when your mother insisted he be your partner."

"Dad, you've trained me well. I have a good partner and a good horse. I'll be just fine. I'm not going to win any wars using brute force, am I? So, intelligence and thinking outside the box are going to be my domain—exactly where Jacques fits in."

"I know but…come on, Katana—" he motioned towards the self-pitying wolf "—since when do wolves have an emotional breakdown because they might not be scary enough?"

"Since when do wolves speak, Dad? None of this life is normal, period, so why do you keep expecting him to conform to what a normal wolf is?"

Malaceia threw his hands up in the air in despair. "Katana, he wears a bib to eat, for goodness sake!"

"Hey," she replied, setting her hands on her hips. "White fur is hard to keep clean. It's hard to get blood stains out of that."

"You're making excuses for him. You know what I'm saying is true."

"I think you're bullying him, actually. You're not being fair. Technically speaking, you're being racist."

Malaceia burst into laughter. "How do you figure that?"

"Because he's not like the others of his kind, you're victimising him. Diversity never hurt anyone. That's how evolution works if you think about it."

"Believe me, sweet girl, there won't be any evolving from his type. If he were human, he'd be in Vegas in sparkly dresses and calling himself Jennifer."

A small whimper sounded from Jacques. Under such brutal scrutiny from Malaceia, it couldn't really be a surprise.

"You're hurting his feelings, Dad. Stop."

Malaceia rolled his eyes. "I can see I'm getting nowhere. The first scratch you get and it's his fault, he's gone and you're off the field. Do you understand?"

Katana stared her father down. She knew by 'gone' he meant dead, and she also knew by 'off the field' he meant getting married and sprouting kids like a battery hen. After a few tense seconds, she nodded.

"Good. I'll tell Sophia to email you your first assignment. I have the perfect case for you."

Squealing in excitement, Katana rushed forwards and hugged her father, thankful that finally, she was being allowed to play with the big boys. This was her time to make a stamp on the hunting world.

2

Less than an hour later, Katana was packing her bag for a trip to Scotland.

"Isn't this exciting, Jacques? It's not quite the European adventure I was hoping for but still, I have my first official case."

"Oui, madame," Jacques replied, not even bothering to take his attention from the TV.

"Maybe we'll get to go abroad on the next case. Maybe I'll finally get to leave England and travel."

"Oui, madame."

Katana sighed at her friend's dismissal of their conversation. There were times when he shut down and refused to engage for no obvious reason. This was one of them.

Looking down into her suitcase, Katana sighed at the bleak colours of the clothes staring back at her.

Having to blend into forests and surrounding foliage left little to the imagination in terms of suitable clothes.

For the sake of comfort, ease of flexibility, and of course the fact most of her time was spent on horseback, Katana's suitcase was filled with dark coloured jodhpurs, dark coloured cotton shirts, and knee-high black riding boots.

For the briefest of moments, she debated what the suitcase of any other twenty-two-year-old girl would look like if they were going away for several days to some place new, like a mini holiday. Colourful dresses, high heels, and make-up would be dominating their bags for fun times and memory making moments.

To lessen the dismal colours saturating her eyes, Katana looked at her red riding cape and her high-neck frilled collar white shirts. They were the official uniform of a Kempe; of a Red Riding Hood.

Up until two hundred years ago, it had been mandatory for all hunters to wear the uniform and hunt with a horse and a dog (now a wolf) in remembrance of Henry.

With werewolf attacks becoming more urban as the population expanded, and also the increase of pesky items like cameras, the uniform law had slackened and was now only required if the hunter had to present before the Preternatural Council.

Riding a horse through woodland and forests wasn't out of the ordinary, and the use of wolves was neither here nor there with civilians more commonly mistaking them for husky breeds or wolf-dogs.

"It's a young girl," Katana said, her voice shaking. "She was eight, Jacques."

Jacques, who was watching a shark attack programme on National Geographic, didn't dignify his partner with an answer until the adverts came on.

"It must have been a new-turn—" he scratched the back of his neck with a back leg

"—that couldn't control his blood-lust. No biggie."

Katana raised an eyebrow. "No biggie? Jacques, this goes against everything we were taught about werewolves. The youngest they kill is eighteen."

Quirking up a furry eyebrow, Jacques simply replied, "Obviously not."

"I wonder if Dad is expecting me to stumble across something big with this. Do you think that's why he gave it to me? He's wanting to help me prove myself?" Katana fumbled around in her pocket for her phone, wanting to call her father. "Why hasn't he made more of a big deal about it though?"

Jacques snorted. "I think that's being a little optimistic. Your father never does anything unless it benefits him in some way."

"True," she said, pursing her lips. "But think about it—there was only aunt Marion hunting until she died. Females out in the field is almost unheard of. Now the big boss has his own daughter wanting to hunt, he's going to want me to be the flagship example for all future Kempe women to follow in this life."

"You have an excellent imagination, K," he said, daintily crossing one front paw over the other. "Have you considered that maybe this young girl isn't the first of her age group?"

Katana frowned. "Are you saying Dad's been keeping secrets from us?"

"No. I'm asking if you've considered that other young children have been mutilated."

"That's the same thing."

"No, Katana, it isn't."

Crossing her arms over her chest, Katana scowled at Jacques. "No, I haven't considered it because I don't need to. If other children had been attacked, then all the hunters would know."

Jacques stared back at her with a poker face. "You're cute."

"Excuse me?"

Jacques was saved from answering as the adverts finished, signifying the switch of his attention back to his shark programme. He raised his nose in the air, pointedly ignoring Katana.

If it wasn't for the fact she enjoyed intellectual conversations, she would have chosen one of the regular brutes to be her hunting companion, but that was something she'd never admit to her dad.

Something about Jacques' implication wouldn't leave her alone. She found herself pondering the question that if this was the first child attack, why wasn't more of a fuss being made?

Irritation sparked inside her when she thought about her dad's reluctance to send her out in the field. What if he was setting her up to fail so he could shelve her from hunting and marry her off to start breeding the next generation of hunters? That is what he'd always tried to steer her towards, after all.

Sighing in exasperation, she pulled her phone out and decided to call Erica, her best friend since childhood. Erica was a witch from the Amethyst Coven that associated with her family.

"Erica Mayweather speaking. How may I help you?"

"Very funny," Katana said. "I'm guessing Bryn is your latest infatuation then?"

Erica giggled down the phone. "Actually, we are going out on a date this evening so there." She stuck her tongue out for extra effect, even though she knew her friend couldn't see it.

"Seriously? You bagged a date with Bryn Mayweather?" Katana couldn't ignore the fact she felt slightly envious because if she ever happened to be interested in the male species, Bryn Mayweather would have been high up on her 'ideal' partner hitlist. Although, if her father had anything to do with it, she'd be married off to Tobias Bembridge, one of the Preternatural Council members pretentious sons.

"Yep. Want to ask me how I got it?"

Katana raised her eyebrows. "Do I dare ask?"

"He had some car trouble. I fixed it. He was so impressed he asked me out to dinner."

"Oh my god," Katana replied, giggling. "Are you kidding me? You're supposed to be the damsel in distress, Erica, not him."

"Hey, it's Bryn Mayweather. I couldn't have cared less if he was wearing bright yellow Speedo's and pink nail varnish."

Katana laughed. Bryn looked like your typical alpha guy in that he had the six-foot height, the broad muscled shoulders, the stern look to intimidate anyone within staring distance, but it was well known he was just a giant teddy bear and a sensitive kind of guy. He worked in childcare for a living, not following his mother's footsteps into being a Council member.

"So what you gotta tell me then?" Erica said.

"Well, I'm off to Scotland on a case."

A gasp echoed down the phone. "No way. He finally let you out on a case? Does that mean he's given up trying to marry you off?"

"Well, I don't know about that. The case is a little…it's got issues. I thought maybe he was trying to help me prove myself, but then Jacques pointed out it's Dad, and well, you know—he never does anything unless it benefits him."

"What's the issues? Anything I can help with?" Erica loved playing with computers and 'accessing' systems she wouldn't normally have permission to access.

"No, not really. It's a little girl that's been killed—she was only eight."

"But werewolves don't kill that young?"

"I know. Jacques kinda implied it's happened before whereas I thought maybe Dad was wanting me to prove myself but now I'm not so sure. Just this morning he had me going through the old 'red riding hood' routine again. I mean come on, I mastered that when I was six."

"Something sounds a little fishy to me. I wouldn't trust that this case is legit, K. Just keep your wits about you, please? And if you want me to, you know, have a look on your dad's computer, just say and I'll be in there like a paedo in a playground."

Katana laughed and shook her head. "You better watch your bad humour around Mr Mayweather this evening or you might be staying Miss Atwood for a while longer."

"Yeah, yeah, I know—best behaviour and all that. What time are you leaving?"

"Altair's already on his way up there so I'd better get a move on myself."

"Let me know if you meet any dashing Scottish men."

"Bye, Erica."

As Katana ended the call, the narrator from Jacques shark programme sounded across the room, "According to recent studies conducted by various universities across the world, sharks are now considered to be more of a social creature than previously understood. Pack hunting has been observed on a number of occasions in many different circumstances."

A cog turned in Katana's head. What if werewolves were no longer hunting alone?

3

Later that evening, Katana arrived at the small hunting lodge her family owned. Nestled right next to Loch Trool in Dumfries, the stunning grey stone building resembled a downscaled castle.

A small round tower housed the front door and a window near the top. To the left and the right of the circular stonework were two regular looking miniature 'wings.' It slept eight people and was entirely self-sufficient with its own hydro-electricity and water supplies, and a fully functioning wood burning stove.

Feeling rather worn out from the travel, Katana rolled her eyes at the orange sunset on the horizon, refusing to give in to her body screaming for rest.

Desperate to make some progress on the case, she pulled out a heart-shaped bloodstone from her hand luggage and closed her fist around it.

As the driver unloaded Altair from the trailer, Katana took a brief moment to close her eyes and feel the power of the stone re-energising her whole body.

By the time Altair clattered off the loading ramp, snorting like a wild mustang, Katana felt like she'd had a power nap.

The beautiful lodge was in the shadow of Robert the Bruce's stone. It was quite a tourist attraction which meant good news and bad news.

It was good for Katana in that she would never be far from help if she was ever in dire need of it. It was also good because it meant it was more than likely the attack happened near the lodge.

However, it was bad news because it meant more civilians could be in harms way. The acres of barren hills, mountainsides, small woodlands, and damp moorland provided the perfect landscape for adventurous hikers—and werewolves.

With hundreds of trees and wild bushes for cover, stealth attacks were going to be an easy feat for any creatures out here. The sparsely populated area meant their tracks would be virtually undisturbed but also hard to find. This was going to be a tricky first case.

Katana waved goodbye to Morgan, the driver who had brought her up here, and saddled Altair up.

From the maps she'd studied on the journey here, they weren't too far from the crime scene. She threw her luggage into the picturesque house, saddled up, and headed out.

With Jacques trotting out in front, picking up the scent of the trail, Katana let Altair pick his way over the rough, uneven ground to find the path better suited for him.

As Altair walked over the summer grass, Katana took a moment to revel in the wild beauty surrounding her. Trees, shrubs, and bushes were in full bloom, colouring the mounds and hillsides with dots of yellows, pinks, and purples.

Katana allowed herself to be lulled into a romanticised setting of riding her horse for pleasure across the remote landscape, the wind in her hair and the evening summer sun warming her skin. It was a small moment of heaven found within a dark foundation.

A large expanse of woodland splayed out across the land in front of them. Jacques headed straight inside the treeline, his nose to the floor and his ears pricked forwards.

"I can smell him already," Jacques said, stopping around six feet inside the treeline. "He's not been gone long. Half an hour tops."

"Great," Katana replied. "Would be a male, wouldn't it?" She sighed as she urged Altair on in the direction Jacques was now going. "Wait, Jacques—isn't the crime scene that way?" She pointed to her left.

"Yes, but this way has the freshest trail. Have you got your bait?"

Katana sighed and rolled her eyes. She reached inside her left-hand saddle bag and pulled out a small spray bottle. She dowsed herself in the scent of freshly baked meatloaf and scowled. "When haven't I?"

They carried on in silence. Katana mused over the basic werewolf bait—meatloaf. It tickled her considerably that a beast so huge and powerful could be lured in with something so trivial. It seemed that old fairy tales did have some standing in their details.

The practicalities of carrying freshly baked goods had been ditched with the compulsory uniform, resulting in a 'perfume' replacing the actual food itself. It worked just as good as the real thing.

As they reached an area where the trees started to close in and block out the dying light, Katana felt her Arab gelding tense beneath her. He stilled and started quivering from head to hoof.

Immediately, Katana drew her wakizashi, the middle sword of her full Samurai set.

Her tanto and her wakizashi were always settled against her right hip whilst her katana nestled in its own vertical sheath just behind her saddle. With its length and how its end dangled below Altair's belly, it always made her giggle as it could easily be mistaken for something else if anyone looked at him from a funny angle.

Jacques froze. His tail pointed out behind him like an arrow as he stuck his nose in the air, twitching it from side to side.

When he realised what he'd caught scent of, he turned to Katana and Altair to shout a warning to them, but it was too late.

A pair of bright yellow eyes were already homed in on their target; the ultimate prize of a female hunter. The bear-sized beast crashed through the trees, running at Altair on its back legs. Both of its black hairy arms were outstretched towards the tender meat sat on the horse's back.

Altair ran towards the huge creature, momentarily startling it. He darted to its left, using the precious few seconds he'd bought to zig zag through the trees like a deer.

Katana stuck to him like glue, allowing her body to relax and flow with his sudden movements. It was an art form that had taken years to master.

When they were hidden from view for the briefest of seconds by a chunky tree, Katana jumped down from Altair, leaving him to carry on through the woods without her.

Blinded by bloodlust, the werewolf ran straight past her, solely fixed on the horse slipping through the trees ahead.

As it hurtled past the tree trunk sheltering her, a gentle breeze slid through the woods, carrying her sweet meatloaf scent right into the werewolf's path.

Katana lifted her sword, preparing to run at the werewolf from behind and deliver a paralysing blow to its spine.

But, it turned towards her at the last second, freezing her to the spot. Its evil beady eyes fixed on its prize and for the slightest of moments, it grinned. White foam hung from its mouth in thick globules, swinging from side to side as the beast galloped towards her.

A white blur dashed through Katana's vision from the right, colliding with the dark monster in a yin-yang mix of mayhem. Snaps of jaws, growls, and angry snarls echoed through the empty area.

Katana snapped back into action. "Jacques, get out the way!" she yelled, running towards the fighting ball of wolves.

A yelp pierced the air. The two wolves parted, flanks heaving as they laboured in their breathing.

Jacques' muzzle and chest were covered in blood. Panic flooded Katana. Had Jacques been hurt?

She dashed forwards to her friend, desperate to save his life.

When the werewolf stumbled backwards away from Jacques, Katana noticed a missing chunk of flesh from its left side, just above its hip.

Still standing on two legs, it looked at Katana and licked its lips. It took one step towards her before yelping in agony and holding the hole in its side with a dinner-plate sized paw.

Seizing her opportunity, Katana ran at the werewolf with both hands wrapped around her sword.

Before the beast could even register what was happening, Katana took a swing at its injury. In one smooth move, she severed the paw holding the wound and made the wound even deeper.

The werewolf howled in pain and fell to its knees.

Jacques bounded forwards and bit down on its good arm, soaking his muzzle in yet more blood.

Katana swung the sword above her head and brought it down across the beast's broad back, splitting its spine in two. Now paralysed and no longer a threat, Katana stomped a foot down on its shoulders, grinning when it shrieked in response.

"Worthless piece of shit," she shouted.

She raised her sword for a final time, ready to take its head, but the beast shocked her by laughing. Its deep rumble reverberated through her body so much, she took her foot off it, startled.

"Stupid girl," the creature growled. "You're just a pawn like the rest of us."

Anger lit up inside Katana. "Fuck you!" With one clean sweep, she cut its head from its body.

Altair picked his way back through the trees just as Katana delivered her killer blow. Blood sprayed him right in the face as he emerged from the trees right in front of the dead creature. He shook his head and snorted before walking to Katana and rubbing his head on her t-shirt.

Katana pushed him off her and went to one of her saddle bags, wanting to find her fire lighting material—the final stage to killing the unsightly creatures.

The key premise from The Red Riding Hood training was that no werewolf was ever dead until the body was burned to ashes—after its heart, liver, and kidneys had been removed and burned in a separate pile of course.

Their taste for liver came from their own regeneration abilities. Nature had enabled werewolves to regenerate their own limbs, head included. It took six days, but the damn freaks could do it, apparently.

Katana had never witnessed it, but she had no desire to either.

Rifling through her saddle bag, she found what she needed and turned around, wood shavings and petrol lighter in hand. She started walking towards the body but had to jump back when it burst into flames on its own.

Altair skittled sideways away from the intense heat. Jacques ran backwards, some of his white fur singed black.

For two or three minutes, thick orange flames devoured the body of the werewolf. Then, just as if someone flicked a switch, a small 'pop' sounded through the air, leaving nothing but peace, quiet, and a small pile of smouldering ash.

"What the hell was that?" Katana whispered. She looked around for Jacques. "Jacques, did you see that?"

The white wolf padded out from the depths of the trees, a pensive look crossing his features. "It would be pretty hard to have not seen it."

"Quit the sarcasm, Jacques, for once." Katana turned and walked back to Altair, wanting her cleaning rag from her saddle bag. She stuffed her fire lighting material back in its home and pulled a blood-stained pillowcase from the leather bag. She wiped her sword clean before re-sheathing it on her right hip. "What the hell was that?"

"If I'm not mistaken, it was a werewolf—"

Katana narrowed her eyes at him.

"Sorry," he said, looking down at the floor. "I don't know would be the answer."

Grabbing her canteen of water hanging from her saddle, Katana took a long, cool drink before resting back against Altair's sturdy shoulder. "Well, I guess there's one thing—we won't be having a mini holiday after all."

4

With her energy levels waning along with the twilight turning into darkness, Katana headed back to the lodge for a good night's sleep.

A post and rail fence lined a decent paddock at the side of the grey stone building for the hunter's horses. A small feed shed at the back of the property housed some hay and straw.

Sheep grazed the lush grass all year round so any horses staying here wouldn't be alone. Being herd animals, they needed the safety of company in order to rest properly.

Katana realised with a grin that if she opened the living room window, Altair would be able to stick his head inside the living room.

After settling Altair for the evening with a decent pile of hay, a feed of warm bran mash, and fresh water, Katana headed indoors with Jacques. She rummaged through the kitchen cupboards, first looking for a sponge and a bucket of some sort, then for some food.

When all she managed to find was an unopened packet of spaghetti pasta and a tin of chopped tomatoes, she put food off for the time being and decided to help Jacques clean the blood from his fur.

Pouring some warm water into the grey washing up bowl in the sink, Katana carried it into the living room and set it in front of the fire.

With the summer sun having set hours ago, a slight chill hung in the air, leaving Katana with no quandary about lighting the fire.

Ten minutes later, hungry orange flames licked the glass windows of the log burner as they devoured the pile of wood stuffed inside.

Jacques laid in front of Katana and the fire, flat out on his side, and closed his eyes. This was a task they both hated but one that needed doing.

The usual process would be Katana scrubbing his fur until he couldn't stand the pulling of his hair roots any longer. At that point, she would then wash his muzzle. After his nose had been scrubbed raw, Jacques would take over and clean himself as best he could.

It often took several days of washing for the blood stains to fade out.

After a good hour or more of scrubbing at Jacques fur, Katana gave in before he did when her stomach started cramping in pain for some sort of sustenance.

More than annoyed all she had to eat would be tomato flavoured pasta, she made a mental note to find out who had last stayed here.

The Red Riding Hoods owned hundreds of properties both in urban and rural settings. One of the steadfast rules of being an active hunter stated that in order to help fellow hunters, the cupboards must always be left stocked up before leaving. It would help anyone staying there in the future if a quick meal needed to be made—like tonight.

Katana picked up the two items that would be her food for the evening and turned to Jacques. "You eating with me or finding yourself something?"

He wrinkled his nose up in disgust at the pasta and ambled out into the darkness, disappearing into the treeline.

Shaking her head, Katana quickly cooked her food, shovelled it in her mouth like she hadn't eaten for a week, and dragged herself upstairs for some sleep.

₧₧

The sound of mumbling voices woke Katana from her deep sleep. When she heard nails scrabbling across the wooden floor outside her bedroom door, she realised Jacques was back, and blatantly not alone.

Grabbing her tanto, the smaller of her three swords, she yanked her bedroom door open.

Jacques stood in front of her door, facing the top of the narrow stairs. With his back up, heckles raised and a deep growl coming from his body, Katana realised he meant business.

When she realised what had him so worked up, she froze.

At the top of the stairs stood a man about her age, give or take a few years. Fair hair, burning green eyes, and a sprinkle of freckles across his nose and cheeks, he definitely fell under the 'eye candy' category.

Broad, muscled shoulders and an athletic body completed the package, but with his stern-faced glare, Katana knew his visit didn't fall under the 'friendly' label.

"Who the hell are you?" she said, raising her tanto in front of her. "And why are you in my house?"

He studied her for a few seconds, roving his eyes up and down her body.

Still clothed in her blood-spattered jodhpurs and t-shirt, she definitely didn't pose as a helpless female. So exhausted from the day's events, she'd collapsed on the bed as she was.

"I could ask you the same question," he replied. "And also why you're covered in blood."

"This house belongs to my family," she said, taking a step forward. "And we don't take kindly to people helping themselves to our property."

"Your family?" he said, frowning. "You're one of the Kempe's?"

Knocked off balance by his knowledge, Katana didn't know what to say. "Yes."

"Who are you exactly?"

"Katana," she replied. "Who are you?"

The guy balked, almost seeming to choke on his own tongue when he heard her name. "You're Katana Kempe?"

"Err…yeah. And you are?"

"Leaving."

With that, he turned around, ran down the stairs and back outside, letting the front door slam behind him.

Katana bolted after him, but with night now truly settled around them, Katana could see nothing but a blanket of darkness as she looked into the bleak environment around her.

Still, she shouted questions into the eerie night time landscape, hoping for answers.

Her answer was silence.

Turning to Jacques, she threw her hands up and said, "What the hell…?"

"I don't know," he said, slinking over to the fire. "I was asleep here and he just barged in and went upstairs."

Katana thought back over what woke her, remembering she heard muffled voices. "You were talking to him. What were you talking about? Do you know him?"

Jacques barked with laughter. "Of course not, don't be silly. I was just telling him to back away and get out."

After a couple of seconds, Katana decided to accept his explanation, even though deep down in her gut, something didn't sit quite right. For now, all she needed was a decent, undisturbed rest.

5

As dawn broke the next day, Katana called her father, gloating at the news she'd already killed her target.

"Really?" he said, disbelief edging his tone. "You got him that quickly?"

"Yeah," she replied, smiling. "Jacques picked up the scent and within five or ten minutes, there he was, coming for us. Jacques took a chunk out of his side, so I made it a little deeper, split his spine, and cut his head off. Job done."

A few seconds of silence followed before Malaceia said, "Well done. I'm proud of you."

"There was a couple of odd things though, Dad."

"Go on."

"Well, first he told me I was a pawn. He said, 'you're just a pawn like the rest of us.'"

Malaceia laughed. "Oh, I wouldn't worry too much, honey. He was just mad he'd been bested by a woman, that's all."

Katana smirked, pride bursting inside her at the fact she'd beaten such a chauvinistic monster. "But then his body burst into flames before I could burn it. It's literally a pile of ash as we speak."

Silence.

"Dad?"

"And you killed him like a normal werewolf—cut his head off and took his organs?"

"I didn't get chance to take his organs before the body burst into flames."

A heavy thud echoed down the line. "Anything else?"

"Well, some guy burst into the lodge last night. It was really odd. He knew it was ours but from what he said, it seemed like he'd been staying here, which considering there's hardly any food in here, would make sense."

"Was this before you killed the werewolf?"

"No, after. Why?" Footsteps in an empty corridor echoed into Katana's ear.

"I've got to go, sweetie. Something's come up. Don't worry, you did just fine. Well done on such a fantastic first case. I'll get Sophia to email you your next move."

"Ok, but Da—"

The ringtone buzzed in her ears. She had wanted to ask him about the age of the young girl and if it was the first of its kind.

What. The. Hell.

⁊⃝⃝

An hour later, Katana still hadn't received her new case details. Bored and restless from the peculiar conversation with her father, she decided to have a look around the stunning scenery before she found herself at the other end of the country, or better yet, travelling Europe.

Saddling Altair up, Katana headed out into the Scottish landscape, Jacques padding ahead of her as normal.

The fact he'd been unusually quiet since last night hadn't gone unnoticed. Katana couldn't help but pay attention to the niggle in the back of her mind that something was…*off*.

As the trio meandered through a small woodland, revelling in the serene beauty of nature at its finest, Altair suddenly stopped dead, refusing to move forwards.

Katana opened her mouth to say something to Jacques, but he had also frozen.

He pinned his nose to the floor as he snuffled through the dirt. "Impossible," he said, lifting his muzzle. "This is the same scent I picked up last night."

Katana's heart dropped to her feet. "What? How is that even possible?"

Jacques turned and looked at her. "I don't know but I'm telling you—this is the same werewolf. And judging from this, he's been through here only an hour ago."

Drawing her wakizashi, Katana dismounted and headed over to Jacques. "That's impossible. I cut its head off. Let alone the fact it burst into flames. You must be wrong, Jacques."

"I'm not. Honestly, the musk coming from that one last night was absolutely repulsive—this is the same."

"Are you sure? What if there were twins? Is it not possible you're confused? I mean, musk is musk and lavender is lavender after all."

"There is no lavender here, Katana, so there are definitely no females lurking around. And as for the scent, you know as well as I do that their scent is as unique as a fingerprint."

She shrugged her shoulders. "I know. I just…with the fact they've killed a minor and all the other weird stuff going on with this case, I'm kinda thinking the general rules don't fit here anymore."

Jacques continued forward, his nose to the ground as he followed the trail. "I'm sorry but there's just no doubting it whatsoever—this is the same wolf from last night."

He picked up his pace and trotted off in front of her, his nose to the floor again like a sniffer dog.

Katana followed him.

She looked back over her shoulder to whistle to Altair but was instead met with a whirling blur of fair hair and green eyes before a sickening crunch threw her into darkness.

6

When Katana came to, she found herself staring up at the grey stone ceiling of her family's hunting lodge. The instant she tried to move, a stabbing pain shot through her temples, causing her to cry out.

"Steady," said a male voice. "You took quite a fall."

She slowly turned her head to the sound of the voice. When the handsome stranger from last night stared back at her, she found herself almost lost for words. Up close, the guy looked like he'd just stepped out of a Hollywood poster.

"Ashley Renata," he said holding his hand out. "Nice to meet you—again."

"I would say nice to meet you but I'm not so sure, especially as you knocked me out." She took his hand and shook it anyway.

He flashed her a toothy grin. "Well, my mum always did tell me I was handsome enough to 'knock 'em out'."

"Think that one would have been better saved for a bar," she replied.

Heat flushed his cheeks bright red. "Sorry. Would you like some water or maybe green tea?"

"No, thank you. Where is my horse and my wolf?" Attempting to sit up again, Katana gave up when blinding pain forced her back down.

"Whatever you've done to my head, it really hurts."

"I'm sorry, I didn't mean for you to hit a rock."

"Oh, but you did mean to rugby tackle me?"

"Well, no, not quite." Ashley cleared his throat. "Your horse is in the paddock, quite safe. Your wolf—well, he's a curious one. He refuses to come anywhere near me, despite my reassurances. He's watching from the treeline I suspect. I can feel his beady little eyes on me even in here."

"How do you know my family?" she asked, remembering last night.

He shrugged his shoulders, pulling his dark green polo shirt tight across his clearly defined chest. "You're not the only hunters in the world you know."

"I'm well aware of that. Just the chances of bumping into another hunter in this particular region are exceptionally small. What do you hunt exactly? What family are you from?"

"Everything."

Katana frowned. She knew there were several families like hers, but they all specialised in specific creatures.

There was no 'multi-genre' hunter—not officially anyway. Those that attempted to hunt without the Council's approval often ended up dead because they lacked the magickal support of a witch coven needed to hunt the creatures.

"You're lying," she said. "There is no family that hunts everything."

"I'm not lying." He walked over to her and helped her sit up. Passing her a bag of towel-wrapped ice for her head, he said, "My family don't want to be too specific; we just want to help. We're awaiting Council approval so we can be given the same distinction as all you big guys. All we want to do is kill the creatures."

"Ok. So what family are you with?"

"Crikey," he said, moving away towards the small kitchen. "Have they brought you back from the Spanish Inquisition or something?

"Knowledge is power, Ashley. I like to know what and who I'm dealing with at all times. Especially when they jump me out of nowhere in the middle of a secluded woods whilst I'm stalking a werewolf with my tanto drawn." She flashed him a sickly-sweet smile.

"You got a boyfriend?"

"I beg your pardon?"

"I said, have you got a boyfriend?"

"I don't see what business that is of yours." More than annoyed, Katana took the ice from the back of her head, noticing the red spots all over the light green towel. Regardless, she put it down on the seat next to her. "Thank you for knocking me out and for the ice and all, but I have a job to do. Good day."

A low chuckle sounded around her as she strode for the door. "I'll take that as a no."

Katana let the door slam shut behind her after she walked out. Scanning the tree-line for Jacques, she didn't have time to spot his hiding place before he was loping towards her, relief written all over his face.

As Jacques closed the distance between them, Katana turned to her right to see Altair tied to the fence of the paddock. She rolled her eyes and tutted in annoyance. Why hadn't he just turned him loose instead of leaving him in the baking heat?

"I was getting worried," Jacques said, finally reaching her side. "That boy has testosterone levels through the roof. He wanted to mate with you."

Embarrassment flooded Katana in an instant. Yes, she was a virgin. No, she didn't care.

With a job like hers, sex and relationships didn't even linger at the edge of thoughts. She couldn't afford to be pulled off track by some hunky guy with romantic notions that would last less than ten percent of her total lifetime. As far as Katana was concerned, she had better things to do with her life and her time.

"Your pheromone levels are suggesting you find him attractive," Jacques continued, padding to her side.

"Cut the science crap for once, Jacques, will you?" Katana jumped up on Altair's back, grateful to see her katana sword hadn't been stolen. "Let's get going. We've lost enough time as it is."

"And where exactly do you suggest we go?"

"Back to where we were. Where you found the tracks and the scent."

"Yes, that's a bit of a problem, actually. Before Prince Charming appeared and bowled you over so suddenly, I'd actually lost the trail myself. It was oddly peculiar. Almost as if someone had picked the damn creature up from the air and lifted him somewhere else."

Katana frowned at him. "Are you sure you didn't hit your head too?"

Jacques rose to his feet and trotted off in the direction from which he'd arrived. Katana shook her head and urged Altair forwards after him.

7

Trekking back into the woodland, Katana pondered over her options. Her father was giving her a new case yet according to Jacques, the werewolf wasn't dead. What was she supposed to do?

The thought of ringing her dad and explaining that the werewolf was still alive wasn't something she particularly wanted to do.

Altair picked his way through the trees, following Jacques' lead as Katana lost herself to her only options; calling her dad, being shouted at and told to come home, or not calling her dad and finding something new and ground-breaking.

Katana grinned. She had a lot of ground to cover to catch up with her brothers and be held in the same high regard as they were.

Brogan, her eldest brother, had been specifically asked for by the Met. Whilst she carried the required happiness for her sibling's success, she also harboured a deep seated jealousy—after all, that could have been her if her father hadn't held her back for so many years.

Jacques stopped and turned to her, sighing. "May I suggest an inspection of the crime scene?"

"For what reason, Jacques? Dad is sending me a new case."

"You and I both know that you're not going to call your dad and tell him about the latest developments and we also both know that you're not going to leave this alone now."

Katana lifted an eyebrow. "Really? And what makes you so sure of that?"

"Because I know you. You're like a damn terrier on a trouser leg when you get an idea in your head."

"I have no ideas in my head."

"Yes, you do. And they all involve images of grandeur and sticking two fingers up to all the males in your family."

Katana laughed. "Ok, guilty as charged. Lead the way."

"Before I do," said Jacques, taking a couple of steps towards her. "Can I just say I warned you not to."

"What the hell is that supposed to mean?"

"If you pull at this thread, Katana, it's going to unravel a whole load of dirt you really wish you didn't know."

When Katana registered exactly what he was meaning by this, she dismounted and walked over to him, her shoulders squared and her hands on her hips. "Are you telling me you know things that I don't?"

Jacques dropped his eye contact to the floor. After a few seconds, he said, "There are a lot of things you don't know. I'm merely warning you that if you chase after them, you will probably end up very lonely."

Katana's mouth dropped wide open. "What are you talking about?"

"I just need to say that when this all meets its sticky end—which it will—your life will never be the same again."

"Why am I going to be lonely, Jacques? Am I that unlikeable?"

"No. But you'll see. You'll have to make choices you never would have considered."

"Right. And you now expect me to not pull at this thread and leave everything alone?"

"Not at all."

Katana narrowed her eyes at him whilst pondering over their conversation.

Jacques wasn't stupid by any stretch of the imagination. The intellectual conversations the pair of them enjoyed were one of the main reasons Katana loved him so much. However, his philosophical turn today only peaked her interest and curiosity, not dissuaded it.

"What are you up to? What are you trying to get me to do?"

"I'm saying nothing more," he said, finally looking up at her. His brown eyes were swathed in sadness. "I'm just telling you your options and what the result of each of them will be."

"Why me, Jacques? Why not Brogan or Ethan?"

The white wolf sighed and sat down. "Because they're nothing but miniature Malaceia's. They don't have the brain power to think outside the box. To put it simply, they're soldiers—they follow their orders and get the job done with no questions asked. You have always asked questions. Why do you really think your father held you back for so long?"

A lightbulb went off in Katana's mind. Slowly, the jigsaw puzzle started piecing together.

The chauvinistic way of their business had always been a key contender for her failure, but with the world becoming more modern and catering more for female equality, Katana had only ever viewed her success as a female hunter as something to strive for; not something that her own father would fear and use against her.

With everything about this case now ringing alarm bells and the odd phone call with her father this morning, Katana knew Jacques was right—her father hadn't put her out in the field because he knew she would succeed, he'd put her out here to scare her into going home and popping out babies.

"So what do I do about the new case he's sending me on?" Katana said, already feeling conspiratorial.

"Call Erica."

Katana gasped. "What?"

"Call your hacker friend and tell her to hack into the mainframe system. Tell her to do whatever she needs to in order to put your tracker in the region of the next case."

Rubbing at the back of her neck, Katana traced her fingertips over her colourful tattoo.

Only around 6 inches high, it was a cartoon drawing of a blonde-haired girl in a blue dress covered over with a red riding hood. Two huge blue eyes dominated her round face with a dark expression oozing from their depths.

All the hunters carried them. The ink had been specially mixed by their coven of witches to include tracking abilities. It effectively acted as a microchip without the cold metal actually being in their body.

"I don't know if that can work, can it? I mean, technology and magic—there is no crossover between them, is there?"

Jacques snorted. "Ask me that in a week's time."

Eyeing him with suspicion, Katana pulled her phone out of her pocket just as it pinged with an email from Sophia. "My new case details are here," she mumbled, scrolling through her last dialled list without even looking at the email. Hitting 'Erica,' she turned her back to Jacques as she listened to the rings baying for her best friend's attention.

"Tell me you want me to hack your dad's computer," Erica said, answering on the fifth ring. Her voice was laced with pleading.

"Yeah…why?"

"He's gone mental in the lab this morning. I mean he literally burst through the door—busted it clean off its hinges—grabbed Gregory by the scruff of the neck and dragged him upstairs. I couldn't hear exactly what they were saying but I heard him mention your name and something about ash."

"Ash?" Katana immediately thought of Ashley, her newly acquired handsome stalker-stranger. "What do you know about him?"

"Who?"

"Ashley."

"Who the hell is Ashley?"

Katana took a moment to explain the odd situation. "Ashley is his name. It must have been him they were talking about." Katana paused. "But I didn't tell Dad his name—I didn't even know his name until an hour ago. Maybe it was the fact I said the werewolf's body had burned to a pile of ash."

"Whatever, chick. If you want me on that computer, I'm on it."

"Yeah, I need you to do me a favour though. Sophia has just emailed me through a new case."

"You want me to relocate your tracker?"

"Will you quit the weird psychic stuff. It's freaking me out."

Erica laughed. "Sorry. I can't help it. Mum's teaching me to expand my thoughts or whatever. We came to yours this morning to give your mum my shielding papers for my exam and I could see what happened like a movie right in front of my eyes. It was fascinating."

"I'll take your word for it," Katana said, laughing. "Let me know what you find."

"Sure thing."

"Oh, and Erica?"

"Yeah, chick?"

"Be careful."

8

"So, I'm guessing we're going this way?" Jacques said, turning in the direction of the crime scene.

"Yes," Katana replied, her tone curt. "Congratulations, Jacques. Whatever little mission you wanted me on, you've manipulated me into doing it."

"K, that's not what I wanted at all. It's just…it's complicated."

Mounting Altair, Katana nudged him towards their new direction. "However you want to put it, Jacques, you know things I don't and you've used that advantage to get me in place for whatever it is you have in mind."

Jacques scanned his eyes across her hard-set face and sighed. "It's about an hour's walk this way," he said, trotting off through the trees. "Have you got your lights with you tonight?"

Looking at the dying sunset, Katana realised they'd be hitting twilight just as they reached the area where the dreadful thing happened.

All hunters possessed a necklace made of Himalayan rock salt crystals, made by the Amethyst Coven.

Whenever she needed light, Katana would take the necklace and simply heat one of the golf-ball sized crystals with a match or a lighter. After a few seconds, the heat and light from that one rock would spread like a domino effect around the rest of the necklace, giving off bright illumination in less than a minute that lasted for hours.

Last night, she'd left it in her luggage.

"Yes, of course. Shall we pick the pace up?" she said.

Jacques nodded and started a steady lope. Altair followed his rhythm, easing Katana into the childhood memory of being on a rocking horse.

The trio cantered on in silence, Jacques leading the way and picking the easiest ground for them to travel across.

By the time they reached the crime scene, about thirty minutes later, sweat coated Altair's neck and shoulders. Jacques, on the other hand, seemed barely out of breath.

Slowing to a walk, Katana dismounted, allowing Altair a brief reprieve. He could have carried on for hours more if needed, but there seemed little point in pushing his limits unnecessarily.

Katana loosened his girth a couple of holes and reached for the five-litre water canteen she kept in one of the saddle bags. She also grabbed the large piece of blue tarpaulin folded into a small square.

When moulded into a concave shape in the top of one of her riding boots, it was a crude but useable way of delivering water to Jacques and Altair when needed.

She removed one of her boots and provided her boys with a drinking source. As they quenched their first, Katana looked around her, trying to get her bearings.

Recognising one of the trees from the crime scene pictures, purely because of the huge chunk of wood missing from its trunk, Katana padded over the earthy floor, dodging sharp twig ends and questionable looking 'mud' with her de-booted foot.

With one boot on and one boot off, she didn't really care for her appearance because considering her surroundings, the chances of bumping into someone were almost zero.

Then again, she'd thought that when Ashley jumped out of nowhere and knocked her out.

Scanning over the ground around her with her necklace of light, she found the compressed area that had been the small girl's final resting place.

Nothing seemed disturbed to give any indication of a fight, but then again in the chaos of a wild landscape, how 'disturbed' would something have to be before it seemed out of place?

"We must stop meeting like this."

The sound of that male voice had Katana standing bolt upright at such a speed, stars danced before her eyes.

No way.

She whirled around to see Ashley stood at the edge of the treeline where she'd left Altair and Jacques drinking out of her boot.

"Maybe you should stop following me," she replied with a sarcastic smile.

"Nice dress code." He winked at her and smirked.

Katana narrowed her eyes at him and crossed her arms over her chest. "What are you doing here?"

He shrugged his broad shoulders and looked over the forest floor between them. "No doubt the same thing you are. Looking for clues. Wondering if the beast has crossed its tracks or anything."

"You're encroaching on my investigation. I don't like it. You need to leave before I call my father and get the Council involved."

Green eyes flashed with anger. In the blink of an eye, Ashley loomed in front of her. His hulking presence backed her up against the tree behind her. His nose almost touched hers. "That would be a very unwise move," he whispered.

"Are you threatening me?" she asked, staring him down and refusing to submit.

"No. I have no need to threaten. I just act."

Katana raised her eyebrows. Daring to make a bold move, she put her hands on his chest and shoved him backwards. Her efforts were wasted. He didn't move an inch.

"Get out of my face before I make you," she said, gritting her teeth together. Katana put her right hand to her side and grabbed the tang of her tanto. Very carefully, she slipped it free from its sheath. Just as quickly as he'd gotten in her face, she poised the tip of the blade under his chin. "I'm not threatening either."

"You haven't got it in you."

Katana inched the blade up higher, springing a drop of blood free. "Try me."

"You have no idea of the can of worms you'd be opening if you killed me, sweetie-pie. It's in your best interests to just back down. Trust me."

Katana barked out a laugh. "Really? Your family, that doesn't even specialise in anything, is so high up and highly regarded that I'm going to regret killing one of their minions?" Katana snorted, her respected seat amongst the elite families going to her head. "I don't think so. You're picking a fight with the wrong person, buddy."

He lowered his chin onto her blade. A thin stream of blood trickled down the smooth silver knife. "About time you came off your pedestal, honey. I know more about your family than you do. I know all of their dirty little secrets. They're so dark and twisted, it'd make your pretty little head spin for days."

Katana couldn't help but falter. She knew her family had secrets; she wasn't stupid. The question was more who the hell was this guy and why was he claiming to know more about her family than she did? She debated his claim for a few seconds before dismissing it.

"You're bluffing. You don't know anything."

The grin that spread across his face could only be likened to something of a psychopath.

"Kill me," he whispered. "Kill me and open the worm can. I dare you."

The idea of killing someone, a fellow hunter, in cold blood didn't sit well with Katana. Yes, they were in the middle of a heated argument, but he sat on her side of the fence—or so he claimed. Why did he want to die so badly? Or was he just trying to prove a point that female hunters didn't have what it takes to match the males?

"See," he said, laughing. "Told you you didn't have it in you."

Katana sneered at him and made a snap decision. "Really?"

Before he could even think of a response, she drove her tanto backwards across his chin, impaling him in the throat. Warm blood sprayed Katana's face.

Ashley's bulky body hit the floor just as Jacques shouted, "No!"

9

"What the hell did you just do?" Jacques said, sprinting over to her. "Katana, you have no idea what you've just started."

Katana looked down at Ashley's body, then back at Jacques. His eyes were wide with fear. Nothing scared this wolf so why did a dead nobody seem to terrify him?

"What do you mean?" she said, wiping her blade against her jodhpurs.

Jacques shook his head from side to side. "I told him this would all go wrong. Arrogant idiot."

"Jacques, what are you talking about?"

Sighing, he sat down and pointed a white paw at Katana to do the same. "It'll just be easier if you sit, wait, and watch."

Katana frowned and sighed. She looked back at Altair to see if he'd finished drinking from her boot. When she noticed him nuzzling across the grassy floor, she took the opportunity to distance herself from Jacques and hobbled over to her boot.

Altair completely ignored her as he continued foraging for berries and nuts—his favourite snack.

Shaking the tarpaulin free of water, she folded it up and slipped her foot back in her boot. A broad grin crossed her face when she realised they hadn't spilled any water in her boot today. If all she gained from today happened to be keeping her socks dry, then it was better than nothing.

After packing her tarpaulin away, Katana looked over at Jacques. She tried to ignore the deep ache in her heart when she took in the sad expression haunting his brown eyes.

Something troubled him deeply but Katana had no idea of his time as a pup with the witches. Perhaps he struggled with the process of transitioning from a wild animal to a domestic servant.

She sighed as she mused over the contemplations running through her mind. Jacques had always been a good friend as well as an ideal hunting partner, even if all they'd hunted up to now had been the werewolves kept on her family's grounds for training.

If something about all these mysterious circumstances meant she could help him in some way, then Katana wanted to do that. She felt it was the least she owed him.

She patted Altair on the neck and hooked his drooping reins around the small horn on the front of the saddle, so he wouldn't get his feet caught up in them.

Deciding to head back over to her forlorn looking friend, she turned around and started walking over. She'd barely taken three steps before a whooshing ball of flames sent her flying backwards, shrieking in surprise.

Altair snorted but barely moved. Some of the things he'd seen and heard during his ten years in this family would have given most horses a heart attack, but to Altair, they were just every day occurrences.

Jacques scurried back, licking at the few more singed hairs along his body.

Acting on instinct, Katana jumped to her feet and drew her tanto, unsure of any threat that may suddenly arise.

She then watched, in awe, as the most amazing thing she'd ever seen unfolded in front of her eyes.

The explosion settled into a circle of two-foot high burning orange flames that enclosed the area where Ashley had fallen.

Katana squinted her eyes, trying to make out Ashley's body. It took her a few seconds to realise he wasn't there. Her heart leaped. Where the hell had he gone?

From the centre of the circle rose a stunning yellow-orange bird. It flapped its huge wings slowly. As it rose higher and higher, a long-feathered tail followed, snaking from side to side.

By the time the arrow-shaped tip of its tail emerged from the flames, its head floated way up in the tree line, easily thirty feet high.

Then, as if someone had suddenly startled it, it gave one huge flap of its wings. A sharp clap, almost like a whip being cracked, echoed around the dull, evening sky. The bird then vanished up into the dying sunset.

Katana let her mouth fall wide open. She looked over at Jacques and said, "What the hell was that?"

"That was a phoenix."

"But…oh my God." She ran over to the circle, the flames now gone. All that remained of its existence was charred, smouldering grass. "Did you know that was going to happen?"

He blasted her with a look of stupidity. "What do you think?"

"I think you need to start talking."

𝔰𝔬𝔠𝔯

Twenty minutes later, Katana sat on the woodland floor with her back up against a tree, waiting for Ashley to arise from the dead.

Jacques had refused to say a word until 'the show was over' as he put it.

She sighed and tapped her fingers on her knee. Patience at a time like this was not something she wished to indulge in, however, she had little choice it seemed.

As if the universe answered her prayers, the ground in front of her started vibrating.

From the blackened ground, almost like something from beneath pushed it through, rose the body of the man she'd driven a knife into.

The flames returned in their heated might. Katana shuddered as the air around her changed, becoming charged with electricity. A rumble from overhead stole her attention to the skies.

She looked up to see the bird from earlier now divebombing at Ashely's body. It moved at such a rate of knots, it resembled nothing but a yellow-orange streak of lightning.

When it hit his body, the flames went out with a whoosh, covering her in chills.

Ashley woke with a choking gasp, like he'd been electrocuted back to life. He took a second to glance around him and then gave Katana a big smile.

"So you do have what it takes after all. I'm impressed."

"Excellent. Now maybe you can impress me and make my 'pretty little head spin' with all your secrets."

10

As much as she didn't want to, Katana had to admit that Ashely's secrets did in fact make her pretty little head spin. What he claimed seemed so outrageous she wouldn't have believed him if it weren't for the fact she'd just seen for herself he was a phoenix.

But that wasn't it.

When he was re-born he carried with him a certain musk that even without Jacques finely tuned nose, Katana could pick up on.

"They were your tracks earlier today, weren't they?" Jacques asked, laid on his belly with one paw crossed over the other. "And last night."

Ashley nodded. "Guilty as charged."

"So what the hell are you?" Katana said, narrowing her eyes at him. She had her tanto in her hands still, just in case. If necessary, she knew she could stick him with it and buy herself twenty minutes of a head-start. "More to the point, how do we know it wasn't you that killed that little girl?" She pointed the tip of her blade at him.

He shrugged his shoulders. "I am a phoenix-werewolf hybrid. You don't know it wasn't me and you don't have to trust me either. I'm not going to sit here begging."

Katana glanced over at Jacques. She hadn't decided yet how his lack of information sharing had affected their relationship.

She was hurt, she knew that much, but how to approach the subject with him was still an enigma to her right now. However, that didn't make him immune from her need to probe information.

"Right, you—" Katana pointed her blade at Jacques "—start talking. Sharpish. I think I've waited long enough."

Jacques met her eyes with a hard, flat stare.

Katana balked. She'd never seen such an empty predatory stare on his face.

"I'm not a wolf, Katana," he said. "And neither are any of the others—not even Dylan or Calhoun. We're all shifters."

Katana's mouth fell open in disbelief. "But the…but the witches…they take you and train you…help you speak…"

Jacques shook his head. "No, I'm afraid not. No wild wolves magickally turned into domestic speaking servants. Every single one of us, even your father's precious Ricaldo, is a shifter."

"But…but you don't shift," she said, trying to process the enormity of what he was saying. "You're always a wolf."

"I know," he said, nodding. "We're stuck like this." He sighed. "We are all Gregory experiments."

Katana gasped, inhaling at such a rate she made herself choke. "Gregory? As in geeky scientist, Gregory?"

"One and the same."

Switching her attention to Ashley, she said, "Did you know this?"

"What answer gives me bonus points?" he asked, flashing her a smile.

"So where do you fit in?"

He stood up and gave an exuberant bow. "I am subject number H5A2."

"Wait, what? You're also a Gregory experiment?" Katana stood up and started pacing back and forth across the damp earth. Looking at her watch, it was close to midnight already and all she'd managed to do was find herself in a deeper hole than before she'd even come out here. "I don't understand this. You're telling me that Gregory has been testing on people. Is that right?"

"It goes way back. Further than you think," Ashley said. "It goes right back to the beginning. Where did you think werewolves came from?"

That stopped Katana in her tracks. "Henry? You're telling me it goes right back to Henry Kempe?"

He nodded. "Werewolves aren't natural, Katana. They're man-made."

"But...but we've always been told..." Katana stopped and paused, sieving through her memories for what hunters were taught about werewolves. "We're told they're freaks of nature. Rabid beasts that feed on people." She frowned. "Are you telling me they're actually people?"

Ashley and Jacques exchanged a glance. Ashley looked back at Katana and nodded. "Yes. Every single one."

Katana looked at Jacques. The fact he wouldn't meet her eye contact told her he knew about this. To say she felt betrayed would be an understatement. "But…how? I get it with Gregory—he's a scientist, he experiments, but they didn't have science back in them days."

"No, they had magick instead. Why don't you take a seat?" Ashley said, motioning towards the grassy floor. "And I'll tell you a story."

11

The Tale of Henry Kempe

*H*enry Kempe was neither ordinary or extraordinary. He found himself stuck in a limbo, in a no man's land in between the two.

Tall, gangly, and with feet big enough to be confused for flippers, Henry muddled through his childhood and teenage years with virtually no friends and little interaction from the rest of his family.

Being the fourth child of twelve, by the time Henry started feeling the depths of despair at his unknown place in the world, his mother was already pregnant with child number twelve and too busy running around after his younger siblings to worry for her eldest boy spending all his time in quiet solace.

When Henry finally hit thirteen, he found himself working in the stables at the court of King John. Whilst the work made sure he paid his way in life, the people he had to work with were not too compassionate where it concerned the weedy, under-muscled teenager.

By the age of eighteen, Henry towered above most in height, but his lack of stature made him as intimidating as a sunflower. As a result, he often found himself ridiculed and the target for any ill feeling to be taken out on.

Growing into his early adult years in such an oppressive atmosphere, constantly overshadowed by his fellow workers, it didn't take much for Henry to soon find himself festering in deeply hidden emotions of anger and hatred.

He longed for something to happen so people would respect him and treat him with the dignity they treated each other with, regardless of social status. But currently, Henry happened to be nothing more than a lowly peasant punchbag who hauled manure from the King's stables.

One June morning, Henry undertook an emergency market run for the cook. As he meandered through the cobbled streets heading for the fishmonger, he noticed a young girl following him.

Before he reached Mr Fish, a small hand curled around his forearm and dragged him into a small alley in between a pub and a stew-house.

"I can make all your dreams come true," the girl said.

Henry looked down at the small female, barely reaching his shoulder in height. Wearing a black riding cape, her clothing and body were hidden from him.

What he could see of her were emerald green eyes full of conviction and strawberry blonde hair tumbling around her heart-shaped face in loose curls. Freckles dotted across her nose and cheeks and her pink lips all but hypnotised him as she spoke.

With the two of them pressed body to body in the tight gap between the brickwork, to any passers-by it simply looked like a dirty peasant being given his jollies for the day by one of the ladies from the stew-house.

Intrigue spurred Henry on with the conversation, although doubts raced through his mind at it being some sort of joke set up by his fellow workers.

"How so?" he asked, studying the girl's smooth, porcelain skin.

"I can make you a hero. Make them all respect you like you deserve." She paused and licked her lips. "I've

been watching you, Henry, and I don't like the way they treat you. You're worth so much more."

Truly captivated by this delicate female, Henry became lost to her—already sold on whatever idea she had in mind.

"I'm no ordinary girl, Henry. Name your greatest desire and it's yours."

"For what price? I have no money. If you'd been watching me, you'd know that."

"I do know that," she replied. "I have no price except you, dear Henry."

Henry frowned, confused. Was she propositioning him? "Me?"

"I am of the same age as you and without a husband. My mother berates me constantly, telling me I am fat and ugly, that no man will ever want me as his bride. She says I am already spoiling my fertile years by not being with child already. I see an opportunity here, Henry, a business transaction that can benefit both you and me."

He thought on her words for a moment, fighting with himself over her sincerity. "If you've been watching me like you say, why now?"

She smiled such a sweet smile, bees from a thousand miles would have mistaken her for nectar. "Because tonight is the summer solstice, Henry, and that means my powers are at their greatest."

"You're a witch."

She nodded, her eyes gleaming with joy. "A very powerful one," she whispered. "My name is Lenore. What do you think, Henry? Can we improve our lives together?"

He wanted to step back, to take a moment to think on this bizarre turn of events, but the small space they were cramped in prevented him from moving anywhere but sideways, back out into the bustling street.

"Where shall I meet you?"

Lenore shook her head and giggled. "I will find you."

Left with only a quick peck on his cheek, Henry was soon alone again and wondering if he'd just imagined the strange turn of events. By the time he collected the goods from Mr Fish and returned to the castle, the cook was squawking for her food and smacked Henry around the ears for taking so long.

Trudging back into the stables with ringing ears and a headache, Henry made his mind up there and then that he was going to get the respect he deserved, no matter the cost.

₭₩₨

It was late that night as Henry walked to his small cot bed; his only reprieve from the cruel world he lived in.

Sat high up in the barn, nestled in the hayloft, he shared his space with field mice, a nest of sparrows, and the odd rat. He climbed the ladder to his bed, and when he saw Lenore's pretty face staring back at him from his bed, very nearly tumbled backwards off the ladder.

"Hello, Henry," she said, patting the bed next to her. "Are you ready for this?"

"What are we doing?" he whispered, checking over his shoulder that the only ears now alert were that of the rodents scurrying across the floor.

"I am going to give you a gift, Henry. First, myself, and then what you have always desired."

Henry swallowed the small dry lump lodged in his throat. "What do you mean when you say 'myself'?"

Lenore shrugged off the long white riding cape she wore. The hood tumbled back from her head, the weight of it pulling the fabric from her shoulders. When it hit the bed, Lenore sat naked in front of Henry, her cheeks flushed pink and her curvy body ready for a man.

"When the moon is at its highest, a wolf will break into the stables and savage the horses. Except this is no normal wolf, Henry. This wolf turned from a human. Only a man can kill it. To be a man, Henry, you must have…" she opened her legs to him "…been with a woman."

Completely dumbstruck, Henry could do little else but follow her lead as she guided him in the essence of being a man. True to her word, after Henry had mated with her, an awful commotion started in the stables opposite the barn.

"Take its head, Henry," Lenore whispered. "It's the only way to kill it. Take my cape. My scent will distract it for a few seconds."

Henry raced outside in his undergarments and Lenore's white cape. He grabbed a pitchfork on his way into the stables and startled at the size of the beast feasting on one of the King's horses.

Almost twice the size of the young thoroughbred it was feeding upon, the creature was a formidable sight. Shaggy black fur covered its entire body and its limbs were taut with defined muscles.

Upon sensing the scent of a female, it lifted its head from its meal and turned to face Henry. It closed its sickly yellow eyes and lifted its ugly, elongated snout into the air, twitching its nose back and forth as it figured out the mix of scents.

Remembering Lenore's words, Henry launched himself at the huge monster, aiming his pitchfork for its neck.

The beast opened its eyes, but it was too late. The tapered points of the pitchfork had already pierced its neck, spraying Henry in its blood.

The creature sprang into action, fighting for its life as Henry held onto the pitchfork. The aggressive movements as Henry dangled off the handle only resulted in a sawing motion, further driving the cold metal into its neck.

When the beast swung around in an effort to fling Henry from the end of the pitchfork handle, it misjudged the width in the stables and caught the handle in the railings covering the windows.

With its weight and momentum, the creature stood no chance as the pitchfork was forced through its neck tissue, almost beheading it in one sweep.

With warm, sticky blood spurting from its neck like a fountain, Henry saw his opportunity to end it.

Using the handle for leverage, he placed his feet against the wall behind him and kicked himself towards the beast's unsightly head. His bare feet connected with its snout, ripping more tissue open on its neck.

As he connected his fourth kick, the King's men and the rest of the stable workers were awake and piling in through the door.

The beast's head rolled from its bloody shoulders, coming to rest at the feet of none other than the Master of the Horse, and the Constable.

Henry stood, labouring for breath, covered in congealing blood in front of an audience who had bullied and victimised him for over five years.

The blank looks on their poker faces revealed nothing of surprise or horror for they were all too dumbfounded to react.

When the body of the beast started withering into that of a human, and the head also started to shrink into the facial features of a man, the onlookers erupted into cheers of ecstasy.

Grabbing Henry, they all but swept him off his feet as they marched him into the castle to be presented before the King and his court officials.

After hearing of the ghastly attack that had taken place in his stables, the King immediately granted Henry his freedom and blessed him with the duty of ridding the land of such wicked creatures.

"For every head you bring back, I shall pay you eight pounds."

An audible gasp sounded throughout the great hall.

"But…your Majesty, that is eight times what I earn now."

"I am aware of that," the King said, ushering Henry away with his hands. "I can't imagine there's too many of these things roaming my lands."

Henry bowed, a lightbulb immediately going off in his head as to what Lenore's next move may be.

Giving King John his utmost thanks, he collected the horse and the swords he'd been gifted as a thank you, and rode out into the night, his pockets heavy with money and his heart full of hope.

12

"So what are you saying?" Katana asked, her mind still trying to shift any notion of the fantastical tale she'd been taught from a young age. "That Lenore created the werewolves to keep getting money from the King?"

Ashley shrugged his shoulders. "What do you think? What would you have done in their position?"

Katana slumped back against the tree trunk, ignoring the rough bark scratching at the back of her skull. "We're not an elite family at all. We're a bunch of peasants that hustled through life as con men."

"Well, that's one way to look at it. But really, who are the fools? Who keeps paying for your services to rid the world of these 'monsters'?"

Katana realised he had a point. Lenore had seen an opportunity and exploited it to its fullest. She'd essentially ensured that her entire lineage would never be out of work. "Who was he? The guy she turned?"

Ashley pulled his lips into a thin line. "He was her father. She found him raping one of her younger sisters and cursed him. Her mother refused to acknowledge what Lenore accused him of, so Lenore sought out her own justice."

Katana gasped, almost choking on her sharp inhale of breath. "But why Henry?"

"She wanted out of the family home and needed money to do it. Picking a servant of the King was the most direct way to achieve her aim."

"So she just used Henry to better her own life? What kind of a person does that?"

"Henry gained greatly from their union. It wasn't all one sided. Tell me, what would you have done if you walked in on your father raping one of your siblings, hmmm? Tell me you wouldn't do the same."

"I'd probably want to kill him, yes, but to actually do it? And drag someone else in on the situation? That's something else entirely."

"Look," Ashley said, folding his arms over his chest. "Until you've been in a situation, don't go making judgements."

"Fine. Tell me where this ended up involving innocent people then."

"In any lifetime there are people who pee you off and make you angry. Both Lenore and Henry had plenty of people they wanted to wreak a little revenge on. Each full moon, Lenore would turn one of them, Henry would kill them, and then they would collect their reward. As time went by, the practice has gone on and on until eventually, no one really has to do anything wrong. They just have one of those faces. Throw into the mix power-hungry kids who let magick go to their heads and boom. You have one big mess."

"Wow," Katana said, curling her top lip back in disgust. "That's fucked up. Why wouldn't you reprimand your kids? Where's the moral compass here?"

"Look, Katana. If they hadn't of done what they did, you wouldn't be stood here today with your privileged lifestyle and your millions in the bank. Maybe it's time to pull your head out of your ass and look at the opportunity it's given your bloodline through the centuries."

Katana's blood boiled in her veins. She clenched her fists but before she could act, Jacques stepped in between them.

"Cool it, both of you," he said. "There's enough going on without you two warring as well."

Katana sighed. "Ok. So what about the Met and the governments? After all, we do cover Europe too. You're not telling me that not one of them doesn't suspect something?"

Ashley shrugged his shoulders. "Why would they? Werewolves are a freak of nature to them remember. An infestation like cockroaches or rats. You're effectively pest control. Just more highly paid."

Jacques spoke up before Katana cut Ashley in half with her words or her sword. "All the government cares about is money. You've heard of all the conspiracies about super soldiers and mind control experiments?"

Katana nodded.

"That was all in an effort to cut back on paying your family. If they created a super soldier to do your job, they could pay them the wage of a regular soldier and save themselves millions of pounds a year."

"Millions?" Katana frowned, the enormity of the situation still not sinking in. "How much exactly are you saying my family is paid, Jacques?"

He cleared his throat. "Well, last year, the foreign aid budget was fourteen billion pounds."

"Foreign aid?"

"Yes. The Department for International Development has many sub-sectors that money is filtered out through. It's the easiest way to lose massive chunks of cash. Do you really think the UK spent forty-six million last year in the Chinese film industry?"

Katana's mouth dropped. "Forty-six million? Is that what my family got paid last year?"

Jacques nodded.

"Shit."

"Exactly. If you adjust the cost over the centuries, it's quite clear to see how the Kempe's have gained their status and their wealth. You do know your father is on Britain's rich list?"

"Err…no," Katana replied, dumbfounded. "I did not know that."

"Yes. He's Britain's number fifty-two."

Katana flopped back down onto the grass. The dew from the early morning damp soaked through her jodhpurs but she was too stunned to notice.

"Do they know magick exists?" she asked.

"The higher up officials do."

"Surely they must know that the werewolves are created by magick? Or at least suspect it."

"Some have their suspicions but that's nothing that a little magick on a full moon hasn't fixed."

Katana balked. "Government officials? Are you telling me that anyone who suspects this—" she threw her hands up in the air "—whatever it is, organisation, is turned into a werewolf to shut them up?"

Jacques just looked at her with that same empty, blank stare.

Katana sighed. What kind of a shady, underhand business was she willingly a part of?

13

"So is Gregory now using science instead of magick?" Katana said.

"Yes. And he's looking at easier methods of 'delivery'," Ashley said.

"Delivery?" Katana shook her head, deciding to ask about that later. "Surely then the real enemy here is Gregory. If he's now using science in place of magick to turn people, that's traceable right? Through DNA and stuff?"

"Bear in mind you burn all the werewolf bodies, where are they likely to get DNA from, sweetie?" Ashley said.

"The people they attack. Like the little girl who was killed up here."

"Sure," Ashley said, shrugging his shoulders. "But what do investigators know about DNA? They rely on their labs to give them results."

"And?"

"And who do you think owns the labs?"

Katana widened her eyes. "No way. Are you being serious?"

"I'm sorry. What part of this isn't serious?"

"Alright, quit the sarcasm." Katana chewed on her lip for a moment. "I don't think I really want to ask this, but I have to. How much of this do my parents know about?"

Ashley rolled his eyes and stared at Jacques. "Is this a normal level of intelligence for her?"

Jacques shot him a filthy glare. "No, but neither is finding out that your entire world is built on lies."

"Hey, jackass," Katana said, standing back up and glaring at Ashley. "I need to know exactly where I stand and what all the facts are, you know, since everything I've ever known is blatantly a bunch of crap."

"Sweetie," Ashley said, giving her a withering look. "Where do you think Gregory gets his orders from?"

"Quit calling me sweetie." Katana stopped for a moment, allowing the penny to drop. "Why would Dad order someone to create a beast that he then has to go and hunt down, potentially risking his life? It doesn't make sense."

"Not ethically, no. But it's good business sense. He needs to keep money coming in. To do that, he needs werewolves to be running rife. To keep your family on the top of their game, it needs to be an ever-changing field of expertise that the governments will never understand, because let's face it—what's more authentic than a family of werewolf hunters that date back over eight centuries?"

"Oh my God." Katana sat back down and bent her knees up to her chest, resting her forehead against them. "I'm a crook. My entire family are nothing but a bunch of lying scam artists. Who else knows? Does my mum know? My brothers?"

Jacques shook his head. "Only the head of the organisation knows, but I suspect your mum knows more."

"But there's technically two heads of this organisation," Katana said, remembering her dad's twin, her uncle Arald.

"Exactly."

"Are you telling me Arald knows?"

Jacques nodded and glanced at Ashley.

"He found out a good few years ago, like nearly a decade ago. He approached my mum for help."

"Why did he do that? Who's your mum?"

"Lenore is my mother," Ashley said, his voice deadpan flat.

Katana gasped. "But her and Arald have been having an affair. That's why Dad and Arald fell out."

Ashley chuckled. "Arald hasn't been having an affair with her. She's his ancestor. That's just icky."

Katana's head was whirling. "But, but Dad said…"

Jacques stepped forward, shooting Ashley a glare to silence his next sarcastic remark. "Your father twists whatever is necessary to suit himself."

"But how is she still alive? That means she's over eight hundred years old!"

Ashely shrugged his shoulders, then nodded. "Yes, give or take a few decades. She traded her magick for immortality."

"Is that even possible?"

"Apparently so."

"And she's still fertile?" Katana motioned her hand towards him. "Because you can't be much older than me, I know."

"Looks can be deceiving," he said, winking. "But yes, you're right. I'm twenty-eight. She's not actually my biological mother though. She adopted me after my birth parents abandoned me on her doorstep in the middle of the night."

Katana ignored the questions she wanted to ask about his childhood, they were irrelevant to the situation. "What were you before Gregory got a hold of you?"

"Just a regular witch."

"Now you're a werewolf-phoenix hybrid that can't die?"

He nodded.

The enormity of those words hit Katana square in the face. Gregory had created a hybrid species that couldn't be killed. That was h-u-g-e. Even if only a handful ever existed any one time, the fact they couldn't die meant her family would be constantly in business.

"You can't die?" she asked, trying to fish to see if he knew otherwise.

"I can't really say I've attempted to take my own life too many times, but I've had my fair share of being trialled on by your mad scientist to say I'm ninety-nine percent certain we can't die."

"We?"

He nodded and frowned at her, like she wasn't quite getting something. "You didn't think I was the only test subject, did you?"

Katana widened her eyes. Her cheeks paled as the vastness of this conspiracy registered in her mind. "Do you know for certain there were others?"

Ashley grinned. "Of course I do. There were twelve of us phoenix hybrids, let alone all the others he'd been meddling with."

"What?" she whispered. "He'd experimented with other hybrids?"

"Yes," he said, chuckling. "My subject number H5A2 had a meaning—Human number five for animal experiment number two. The second animal he had been toying with was the phoenix. Hence, here I am."

"What was the first?"

"Vampires."

Katana almost choked. "Vampires? Are you kidding me? He took one blood-thirsty monster and merged it with another?"

Ashley just stared back at her, his face completely blank and impassive.

"Were there any other animals?"

"Well, yeah," he said, nodding. "There were seven animals he tested."

"SEVEN?"

He nodded.

"How many were there of each?"

"There were twelve test subjects for each."

Katana balked and stumbled backwards as if an invisible force had slapped her in the face.

"That's over eighty experimental hybrids." She pondered over this for a few seconds before a more disturbing reality struck her. "You said about easier delivery methods. Does that mean you…they can turn people?"

"Well, yeah. Obviously."

At hearing his snarky tone, she turned on him in an instant. "Obviously? I'm sorry, what part of this is obvious exactly?"

He backed away from her holding his hands up in a surrender sign. "Sorry. I didn't mean to patronise or anything."

She gave him the evil eye before she started trying to make sense of all this. "So, let me break all of this down—just so I know I've got it all straight in my pretty little head." She sneered at Ashley. "Henry Kempe did exist, and he did in fact kill a werewolf."

Ashley nodded.

"The werewolf was created by a witch called Lenore and after the success of the first killing, she turned more men into werewolves in order to keep money coming in from the King."

He nodded.

"The King obviously told of the arrangement to his court and then what? It's passed from throne to throne until the government was eventually formed?"

"Pretty much."

"To piece it all together, some sort of fantastical tale was woven and told down the line until we end up with me, here today. And at some point, Lenore faded into the background?"

Another nod.

"And then…what? Science came in where?"

"Well, if you think about it, science and magick are actually kind of very closely related. It's just science is more to do with what you can physically see and handle in front of you, whereas magick is more about the invisible energy living around us."

Katana gave him a cool, blank stare.

"Ok, sorry. Some of Lenore's children carried on, keeping the werewolves alive and all, but things happened over the centuries—some of their own were attacked or murdered, so gradually the witches stopped wanting to help. With Mum immortal but dried up of magick, no witches were willing to turn people through magick, even if it meant keeping food on the table."

"I'm still waiting for a timeline here."

"Alright. Science replaced magick only very recently. Like in the last few months."

"So it's all been magick up to then?"

He nodded.

"So how has science now replaced magick?"

"Gregory created a virus. A physical illness if you like that can be passed from person to person. It's now reality, with us hybrids, that werewolves can turn people from a bite."

Katana frowned. "That's always been the reality."

Ashley shook his head. "No. I'm afraid it was all a lie. If you're turned by magick, that doesn't then give you the power to turn someone else. You still need a witch."

Katana sat back down, her mind spinning. "So literally, every single werewolf until the last few months has been the result of magick? Not one of them has bitten someone and turned them?"

"Correct. When the witches started refusing to help at the beginning of the year, Gregory began turning people with injections. He had them abducted, brought to the lab, and then released after they'd been turned. But now he's created a virus that will save all that leg work."

"Oh my God. That's crazy. Isn't there someone we can talk to about Gregory? Like his parents or any siblings?"

Ashley looked at the floor. His cheeks flushed a deep shade of red. "He…Gregory is technically my brother."

Katana froze. When she spoke, the high pitch of her voice could have shattered glass. "Say what now?"

"Well, Lenore is his mother, biologically, and I'm her son, legally, so…"

"So there's no 'technically' really, is there? He's your step-brother. Right, do I dare ask how old he is?"

Ashley mumbled something under his breath, still staring at the floor in shame.

"SPEAK UP, ASHLEY. I CAN'T HEAR YOU."

"He's one of the originals from Henry and Lenore. The youngest."

Katana gasped. "So he's immortal too?"

Ashley dared to look up at her. "No…more like living off borrowed time…"

Then the penny dropped. Really dropped. "The first werewolf, Lenore's father, he went after a horse, not a person…when did werewolves start going after people?"

Silence.

"I'm guessing right around the time Gregory decided he wanted to live longer?"

Silence.

"Do werewolves really need the organs they take?"

More silence.

She looked at Jacques. He dared to meet her eye contact for a brief second before looking away.

"Wow. You really must have loved the lie of the life I thought I was living, Jacques, hmmm?"

He said nothing, still looking far away into the distance.

"And to think all you ever did was preach the moral high ground. You're a hypocrite. A really bad fraud. You know that?"

He still ignored her.

Ashley attempted to step in and stood in front of Katana. "Lay off him a little. He's got his own politics with your father that put him in a sticky situation."

"Well, I guess you would know."

Katana wandered off to Altair, needing a reprieve from the intensity of the situation now surrounding her. He stood on the edge of the treeline, nodding off under the full moon highlighting the scenic woodland around them.

With everything she'd ever known now suddenly in tatters around her, Katana had no clue where to turn or what to do. Everything she'd been trained on, trained for, was all just a lie—a big, money-making lie.

14

Malaceia paced back and forth in his office. He'd just spoken with his stubborn as a mule daughter.

She was delighted with the fact she'd killed a werewolf already, but a whole host of issues had happened that should have had Katana running for home, not asking questions.

On a fury ridden impulse, Malaceia stormed downstairs into his basement, the laboratory, and grabbed his scientist, Gregory, by the scruff of the neck.

"Why the hell are werewolves burning into piles of ash before we burn them?" he said, all but growling into Gregory's ear.

Gregory, still shocked by Malaceia's sudden attack, said nothing. He still said nothing even as Malaceia dragged him upstairs and threw him into his office.

"Start talking," Malaceia yelled, slamming his office door shut. "And fast."

Tall, lanky, and sporting the general look of a modern day 'geek' with black, thick-rimmed glasses, Gregory simply smiled and lazily dropped himself into one of Malaceia's leather chairs. "Well, I had a little problem with the phoenix hybrids."

Malaceia raised an eyebrow. "And you thought to only tell me this now?"

Gregory shrugged his shoulders. "I've been busy."

"What problem exactly?"

"Well, they kind of can't die."

Malaceia's mouth dropped wide open. "They can't die?"

"Nope. Tried everything. It's obviously fruitless to burn them because well, they're a phoenix. They thrive on fire."

"Right…so do you want to explain to me how the hell Katana has just come across one in Scotland?"

Gregory gave his shoulders a nonchalant shrug. "Probably because I let them loose."

Malaceia leapt across his desk and grabbed Gregory around the throat. "You did what?"

"I figured it'd keep the hunters busy and maybe they'd become a little creative and fix the whole 'cannot die' issue for us."

Malaceia tightened his grip around his ancestor's thin throat. "Are you freaking kidding me right now? You let all twelve go?"

Gregory opened his mouth to speak but couldn't because of the grip Malaceia had on him. Gregory tapped Malaceia's hand and pointed to his moving lips. He gasped for air when Malaceia finally let him go. "Yes. A couple of days ago. They're all different. Some burst into flames, others don't. There's only one that seems to be a true werewolf-phoenix hybrid— Ashley. I sent him to Scotland on purpose."

Malaceia raised his eyebrows. "Go on."

"I knew that's where you'd sent Katana, so I sent Ashley there."

"You better tell me why before I bust your face."

"You wanted her scared and sent home to marry Bembridge. With the case details already being so odd, it made sense to add a little more...drama. I was also curious for a weakness. Both the phoenix and the wolf are highly monogamous animals. Once they mate, that's it for them. I think it's their weakness—that could be our 'in'."

Malaceia pondered his statement for a few minutes and backed away. "What are you saying?"

"Well, I gave Ashley an interest...Katana."

Malaceia narrowed his eyes. "And what makes you think he'll even want Katana?"

"Maybe because I told him that she's his mate."

On instinct, Malaceia drew back a fist and punched Gregory square in the face. The weedy man's nose burst open, blood flowing like a tap. The force from the punch knocked him across the room, leaving him scattered across the floor.

"A little warning might have been nice, or maybe even my approval, Gregory. You've overstepped a line here. I'm not impressed." Covering the distance between them in two strides, Malaceia grabbed Gregory by the neck of his white lab coat and lifted him off the floor. "You're disrespecting me, Gregory, and it will not be tolerated. Do you understand me?"

With a simple smile, Gregory said, "Sure. But let's not forget who put you at the top to begin with, hmmm? I mean, if it weren't for Mum and Dad in the first place, you wouldn't even exist."

Malaceia let out a shout of frustration and threw the gangly man across the room. He hit one of the mahogany bookcases and crumpled into a heap on the floor. "You can't pull that every time and get away with it. You could apply that to anything in this world."

Gregory stumbled to his feet and brushed himself down with one hand, pinching his nose with the other. "The thing is, Malaceia, most ancestors are in the past. Dead and buried, long forgotten. As you're well aware, I'm not. Now, as you're technically my however many greats nephew, that makes me your elder, which means some respect is automatically commanded. Wouldn't you agree?"

A sinister smile crossed Malaceia's broad face. "No, actually, I wouldn't. Especially when you're only here because you're living on borrowed time. If it weren't for the fact I'm so heavily implicated myself, I'd have turned you in to the Council long before now."

"Ahh, the Council. Yes, the mightiest powers that wield over us and our fellow elite hunting families. Tell me, do you think we have no influence with them?"

Malaceia narrowed his eyes. "Oh, I have no doubt about it. The question is how much influence compared to the other Council members."

The two men stared each other down for several fraught minutes. Eventually, Gregory conceded. "What do you want me to do?"

"I want you to keep me updated on everything that goes on in your freaky little lab."

"Done."

"Gregory, did you even think about the fact that you've gone and put my daughter, the one who always asks questions about everything, in the middle of all of this?"

Gregory gave a thin smile. "Oops. My bad." He didn't like to share with Malaceia *how* the mate of a phoenix hybrid would be a weakness.

15

Past one a.m. and with a head full of jumbled questions, Katana called time on this confession session she'd found herself in. She jumped up on Altair and urged him forwards in the general direction her instincts told her to go.

So annoyed and feeling betrayed by Jacques, she didn't care if she ended up lost; she just needed to move and help soothe the restless energy refusing to settle inside her.

Katana didn't care for the fact that Ashley trudged alongside her, quiet and lost in his own thoughts. She realised, as they picked their way through the undergrowth, that he still hadn't told her exactly what he was doing out here.

"You still haven't told me why you're out here," she said, looking down at him from her position on Altair. "I know the whole hunter thing was a lie."

A bolt of tension ran through him, pulling his shoulders square and clenching his jaw. After a few tentative steps over a soft patch of mud, he cleared his throat and replied, "Gregory sent me out here."

Katana felt like she should have been surprised, but after learning what she had already, it washed over her like another trivial fact in a web of lies. "For what purpose?"

"Well, um–" he lifted a hand and scratched the top of his head "—technically speaking, for you."

That warranted being still. Katana brought Altair to a halt and glared down at Ashley. "Excuse me?"

Ashley took a good few seconds before he looked up at her. When he did, his eyes burned such a fierce emerald green, what he said next almost became of complete inconsequence to her. "Well, Gregory thinks the only thing that may kill us, that our only weakness, is a soul-mate. He didn't quite prepare me for you though. He just said I'd know you when I saw you."

Silence hung in the air. So astounded by this matter of fact admission, Katana didn't quite know what to respond with. After a long, drawn out minute, she finally whispered, "What?"

"Gregory told me that you're mine. He found out what case you'd been assigned to and sent me here first. I...I was tracking the werewolf that killed the girl—that's why Jacques picked up on my scent. He'd ripped out my heart and killed me about fifteen minutes before you arrived."

Katana leaned on the small horn at the front of her saddle. Frankly, she needed the support it offered, no matter how small. "Soul-mate?" As the words left her mouth, Katana found herself giggling. After a few giggles, she erupted into splutters of laughter. "How ridiculous. This isn't some fairy tale."

"No, but I assure you it's very real."

"Of course it is," she said, snorting. "What are you expecting? That I'm going to kiss you, see stars and love hearts, and confess my undying love? Pah!" She nudged Altair forwards, shaking her head. "Nothing but absolute bunkum."

"Really?" he said, shouting after her. "Bunkum like the marvellous little story you've been brought up believing?"

"Hey." She pulled Altair back to a halt. "Just because my entire belief system has now been uprooted and scattered into a million pieces, that doesn't mean you can start manipulating your own shit into my head in an effort to make me believe what you want me to believe. From now on, this is a seeing is believing life for me."

"I'm glad you said that." He stopped at her side and reached up with both arms. With his six foot plus height and Altair's pony sized frame, Katana was easily within his reach. He grabbed her face with both hands and pulled her down to him.

Before Katana knew it, his lips were on hers and she found herself lost to the odd romance of it all. Stars and love hearts weren't present beneath her closed eyelids, but Ashley's voice, his thoughts, and his memories were.

Everything about him as a person danced around in her mind. Images of him in pain, trapped inside Gregory's lab, flashed in her mind's eye. Then, passing moments of blood covered scalpels and various metal instruments, screams of agony, glimpses of others all subjected to the same. Everything of his horror inside that lab poured into her mind like a waterfall.

When Ashley broke their connection, she almost fell from her saddle. Full well knowing what he'd done to her, he caught her and helped her sit back upright. He said nothing, aware she needed time to process what had just happened.

Jacques padded up behind them and growled. "Some warning might have been nice."

"Oh, quit your whining already," Ashley said. "You're like a love-sick puppy."

"Give me an excuse to rip your throat out—I dare you."

"You can rip it out fifty times over, but I'll come back each and every time."

"Doesn't mean I won't enjoy doing it again and again."

"Hey!" Katana said, finally snapping back to reality. She turned in her saddle and glared at Jacques. "What the hell is your problem?"

"Oh, I don't know. Maybe Prince Charming here thinking he can just wade on in, spout off a load of lovey dovey trash and then kiss you without even asking permission."

Katana's jaw dropped. "What on earth crawled up your ass?" The memory of the previous night when she awoke to voices in the cabin sprung to mind. "That reminds me. Were you two talking last night in the cabin before I woke up?"

Silence.

"I'll take that as a yes, shall I?" Katana glared at Ashley and then back at Jacques. "Is there something else I need to know? Did you know what he was here for?"

Jacques hung his head and stared at the floor. "Yes. I didn't want him anywhere near you."

"Why? What threat is he to you?"

"You're mine," Jacques cried. "Not his. Mine." With that, he bolted into the dark forest, his white fur quickly becoming lost to the shadows of the night.

Katana turned to Ashley. "What the hell?"

"Don't you get it?" he said, giving her a look of exasperation. "He wanted you for himself. He's a regular guy trapped in the body of his shift animal, forced to hang around with you day after day. What do you expect from him?"

"'Forced to hang around with me?'" Katana snorted. "Thanks. I'm guessing you've forgotten it's his job to hunt these damn things with me?"

"Job or not, it doesn't make the truth of it all any easier to accept, does it? I mean, have you seen you?"

"What exactly does that mean?"

Ashley face-palmed himself. "I'll chalk this down to being overwhelmed rather than having a specific moment related to your hair colour. He wants his own happily ever after with you, Katana. That's why he doesn't want me hanging around, staking a claim."

Anger sparked inside Katana like the first strike of a match. "I'm not a possession, some toy that you can both fight over. I'm a person with my own feelings, opinions, and views. You're both just as chauvinistic and pig-headed as my father. I'll be damned before I end up with another version of him."

"Like it or not, sweetheart, that's the world you live in. You live in a world where men rule, and women are subservient. Maybe not as much as they were, but they still are. You can't expect rules from an outside world that you don't belong in to filter in here and change everything. It's not going to happen. The success of your family business depends on the men doing their job. That means having a supportive woman at home. Like it or not, that's your life."

Katana snorted. "It's damn well not going to be. It's about time something around here changed and seeing as no-one else wants to bother with it, I'll do it."

As she nudged Altair forwards, another piece of the jigsaw in her head clicked into place. *This* was what Jacques had wanted—he'd wanted a change, knew it needed to be changed, and he'd pushed Katana in the right direction to getting something done.

Like or not, she'd been manipulated in some way or another to do exactly what someone else wanted.

16

Considering the turmoil of the day, Katana fell asleep relatively easily. When they arrived back at the lodge, close to two a.m., she unsaddled Altair, shoved him in the paddock, and stormed upstairs to bed, slamming the door shut behind her.

Ashley set about lighting the fire and curled up in one of the small flower-patterned chairs, accepting of the fact he was not going to sleep well. He didn't want to even risk going upstairs in the fear he might lose his head; literally.

He finally nodded off but was soon jolted awake from a sharp bite to his right knee. When he opened his eyes, he cursed out loud when he saw Jacques staring back at him.

"Outside," Jacques said. "Now."

"Oh, come on, man. We've all had a long day. Let's just leave it for now, hmmm?"

Jacques lunged forwards and bit him again; harder.

Ashley yelped in pain and grumbled his agreement to going outside. Fighting a wolf after such a day and little sleep didn't score too high on his 'want' list but if needs must then needs must.

"Shut the door behind you," Jacques said, padding out onto the grassy ground. The moonlight faded overhead, ready to give way to dawn and a new day. "We don't want to wake her again, do we?"

Rolling his eyes, Ashley closed the door behind him and strolled out into the chilly early morning air.

Altair, munching through his haylage, kept an ear focused on the two beings stood in front of his paddock.

"Right, come on then," Ashley said, sighing. He patted his left shoulder with his right hand and leaned over. "Give me your best shot."

Jacques gave him a withering look and snorted. "I don't want to fight you, you imbecile. I want to talk to you."

Ashley stood back upright, surprise filtering through his sleep deprived eyes. "Oh. What about?"

"Not a word of this to Katana. Do you understand?"

Narrowing his eyes, Ashley looked at Jacques and said, "Well that depends."

Jacques flew at Ashely with such force, his lithe body managed to knock the man off balance, sending him crashing to the earth. The thud he hit the earth with made sure he lost his breath for a good minute.

Stood with a paw on each shoulder and his nose touching Ashley's, Jacques said, "No, it depends on nothing. This is between me and you. Katana doesn't need anything else on her plate at the minute. Are we clear?"

Seconds of silence ticked by as Ashley regained air in his lungs. When he finally got his strength back, he sat up, pushing Jacques off him. "Fine. But only because I agree Katana has enough on her plate. What do you want?"

Sitting down a few feet away, Jacques sighed and said, "Does anyone in your family have any powers left?"

Ashley frowned. "You mean magickal powers?"

"No. I mean psychic powers," Jacques replied, his voice laced with sarcasm.

"Don't get narky with me, lover boy, because it really won't work well in your favour."

Jacques narrowed his eyes and growled. "You know what? Forget it. This was worse than a bad idea. I can't believe I was even stupid enough to think that you might have a wish to help anyone but yourself." Jacques turned and walked off but threw a steely glare back at Ashley over his shoulder. "You can bet your sorry ass I'll be waiting for you to make one slip up, just one, and I'll be in there faster than a bolt of lightning letting her know."

Ashley pursed his lips, then let out a shout of frustration. "Alright, I'm sorry. What do you want to know about my family's magickal powers for?"

Jacques stopped dead in his tracks. He debated over his options for a brief minute. There was no point in going to the coven attached to the family business—they were paid by Malaceia and would be loyal to him until the end.

Even though Erica was Katana's best friend, Jacques still didn't want to risk her knowing too much and accidentally letting something out. It was common knowledge she was still learning her powers and shielding techniques. Realising that actually, his bad idea was the only idea of answering his question, he turned around and ambled back over to Ashley.

"I wanted to know if there is any way Gregory's work can be undone," Jacques said.

"Undone? As in reversed like it never happened?"

Jacques bit back the sarcastic reply he wanted to respond with and simply nodded.

"Are we talking for you, for someone else, or for everyone? Are you trying to figure out if there's a way to kill me?" Ashley peered down at him with suspicion. "Because I can tell you now, that man tried everything he could think of to kill us, and nothin—"

"I mean for me, you self-absorbed idiot."

Ashley fell silent for a second, ignoring the urge to violently answer the wolf's curt insult. "I don't know. I'd need to know the details of how he made you...you, if that makes sense? Was it all science or was there some magick involved?"

"Honestly, I couldn't tell you. I was so young and whacked out on sedatives most of the time, life was just a great big blur back then. Until she came along."

"Who?"

"Katana."

Ashley rolled his eyes. "Please, man. Cut the love crap. It's making me feel ill."

"I didn't mean that. Katana was the one who let us all out. How else do you think we escaped Gregory's insufferable prison?"

"She what? You got out?"

"You really know nothing, do you?"

"What gives that away, hmmm?"

"Alright, time for me to tell you a story." Jacques motioned to the compacted earth floor in front of him. "Take a seat."

17

The Sad Tale of Jacques Dubois

*J*acques Dubois was born in 1991, the sixth child of what would eventually be a family of nine children. The fourth son, he had no real standing in his father's eyes—he was neither the firstborn nor the lastborn, and he was neither the first son, nor the last. Jacques, for all intensive purposes, was just another child to add to the list of Ava and Hugo Dubois; another child to prove how fertile and fruitful Hugo Dubois was.

Ava was an attentive mother and took great care in schooling all her children herself. But, as is often the way with any mother, the youngest children, especially when they are still babes drinking from their mother's breast, will naturally receive more focus than the elder children.

With Jacques being an adventurous, curious child, this would work against him. His natural need to delve into everything and sneak off into places he really shouldn't go would eventually land him in big trouble with nosey men from the neighbouring village of Dalmellington.

The village folk knew that people lived in the wild woods, and they also knew the truth of the people that lived in the woods; the dark secret of the creatures they could turn into.

For young shifters, their strongest night to turn was that of a full moon, but even then, they couldn't draw the power they needed until they turned thirteen.

Unfortunately for Jacques, the night of his thirteenth birthday would be the beginning of a sad life for him.

Excited to be finally like his dad and able to shift into a powerful wolf, Jacques practiced his turn several *times in front of his delighted family. Finally feeling like he had his father's approval, Jacques was pumped full of joy.*

Not far from their home in the woods stood a great hilltop that overlooked a beautiful valley. Being born and raised inside the vast expanse of Galloway Forest Park gave Jacques the ability to not only admire such stunning scenery but also know the best places to view them.

Under that night's full moon, Jacques knew if he stood on the particular hilltop he had in mind, he would be able to fulfil his lifelong dream of being the perfect silhouette of a wolf howling in front of the moon.

Urged on by nothing but that ideal, Jacques galloped off to his perfect setting when his parents started putting his younger brother and sisters to bed. Keen excitement rose inside him, eager in his new mission now his father had been impressed.

What Jacques hadn't considered was the men from Dalmellington knowing when the shifters were most likely to turn, and also using that same hilltop as a vantage point to spot such a feat.

Dalmellington had grown from a small hamlet into a village over the centuries, all of its inhabitants accepting of the fact they lived in peaceful harmony with the beasts in the woods. They did not bother them and vice versa.

However, that didn't mean that rumours of magickal properties coming from such people weren't rife.

To the village folk of Dalmellington, to catch one of these shifters would be fulfilling an ancient prophecy that promised untold riches and fortune for the native families from there.

Aware that one adult shifter was more than a match for twenty human adults, ten men banded together and decided they could take on a child between them; all they had to do was watch and wait.

Unbeknown to Jacques, the men had already spotted his eldest brother Louis, who had been running over the landscape chasing deer.

Louis had been caught but after biting one of the men, had managed to break out of their flimsy net. As Louis fled back home to warn his father of the danger, Jacques was already on his way out to the hilltop, only a mere two miles behind his brother as the crow flies.

Jacques reached the hilltop and took just a minute to gain his breath. Then, with the full moon bearing down on him in all her silver glory, he closed his eyes and imagined himself changing form.

Just as he'd done several times that night already, his body moved with such fluidity, the transition was all but painless. And there, just as he imagined, he stood at the peak of the hill and bayed to the moon.

Lost in his echoing howls, Jacques didn't hear the quiet breaths of the men in the treeline. They'd been about to pack up and go home, figuring it best not to anger the people from the woods anymore, but then, as if their very prayers had been answered, there had appeared Jacques.

As they watched Jacques tilt his head up to the lunar delight on display, they quickly picked their way across the dewy grass; two nets, two ropes, and two pitchforks in hands. Before Jacques knew what was happening, a rope tightened around his throat, cutting off his joyful howl. Another rope gripped the base of his tail, painfully seizing him to the spot.

One man stuck his pitchfork against Jacques' ribs, warning him to behave. Within ten seconds, the happy thirteen-year-old shifter boy had been caught and detained by the people of Dalmellington.

Shocked and stunned, Jacques didn't fight. The biting agony from the rope around his tail was enough to freeze any escape attempts. The humans had learned their lesson with Louis it seemed.

Jacques was taken to the village hall and down into the cellar they used as brief holding cells for any unruly citizens. The men stood guard, all ropes, nets, and pitchforks in place, until the message for their generous donator was delivered.

Offered little water and no food, Jacques only grew weaker and weaker throughout the dozen hours he was held prisoner.

When a booming voice of authority bounced off the walls around him, Jacques knew something had been planned for him. The question was what.

Through sleep-deprived slits of his eyes, Jacques made out the bustling figure of a man over six feet tall and with muscles that bulged like rocks. His entire demeanour screamed power and Jacques could do nothing but wait for his sentence to be heard.

"Excellent catch, men," the man said, striding up to the iron railings keeping Jacques contained. "I have paid your Mayor already. Well done. I can take it from here."

The men bowed and mumbled their thanks before rushing upstairs to their fruits and riches. The man unlocked the heavy chains keeping the railings closed and marched over to his prize. In his right hand he held a needle and syringe.

"Now then," said the man, patting a weakened Jacques on the muzzle. "I think we're going to become great friends. My name is Malaceia and I have an excellent job waiting in England for you." He lowered his hand to Jacques neck, tilting the needle towards him. "Just a quick pinch and it'll be a nice long sleep for you."

Jacques yelped as the needle stuck his skin but then succumbed to darkness.

ഔരു

When Jacques woke again, he found himself underground. The damp earthy smell filtering through his nose told him this along with the lack of windows and the poor light served by candles and a handful of questionable filament lamps.

He scrambled to his feet, surprised to see he'd shifted back into a boy. He was inside a small cage made from steel railings. If he held his arms out straight, he would be able to touch the sides all around him. To his left and his right was an endless line of similar cages, all with young boys trapped inside.

The boy in the cage to his left whispered, "Hey, I'm Dylan."

Jacques turned to him, surprised to see the blank emotion covering his dark eyes. "Jacques. What is this place? Where are we?"

"England. This is some kind of freaky lab. Don't make him angry."

"Who?"

"Gregory. He'll hurt you, real bad."

"Who's Gregory?"

A door slammed shut. Dylan jumped and bolted to the back of his cage. He pressed his right index finger to his lips in a shush motion and stared forwards.

Footsteps echoed across the white tiled floor making it hard to pinpoint where they were originating from.

At the edge of the dim light, in the dancing shadows from the candles, Jacques could just make out the tall, gangly figure of a man in a white lab coat. Thick, black rimmed glasses framed his face and the stern look set on his features told anyone within a hundred-yard radius not to pee him off.

Jacques scuttled back in his cage when he realised the man was heading straight for him.

"Lovely," the man said. "You're awake. I'm Gregory." He wrenched open the door to Jacques' cage and stuck his arm in, reaching for Jacques. "No need to be afraid. I don't bite." Gregory chuckled. "Well, unless you make me."

Jacques pressed himself against the steel railings, trying to stay out of Gregory's reach, but it was fruitless. Gregory had made these cages with the intention of being able to reach every part of them with just an arm. He'd learned long ago not to stick his head and torso in the cage as well.

Before he knew what was happening, Gregory had a hold of his left ear and yanked on it, forcing Jacques to follow the movement.

"Don't be awkward, now. The others will tell you it only makes it harder on you."

Jacques looked across at Dylan. The other boy quickly glanced at Jacques and nodded before returning his deadpan stare back to the front again. It was at that point Jacques decided to just play quiet and follow what was being asked of him.

Gregory walked quickly through the dimly lit room. When he reached a single personnel door, he yanked it open and shoved Jacques through into another small room, lit only by a single, low powered light bulb. Three strides across this cold tile floor, up a set of stairs, and there was another door. This time when Gregory opened it, the bright light that streamed into Jacques' eyes almost blinded him.

The cold, clinical feel to the lab chilled Jacques to the bone. The steady whirring and humming of machines filled the silence. Gregory hurried Jacques down a narrow aisle between several tables of test tubes, microscopes, and robotic arms.

When Jacques saw the big black leather chair facing him, panic immediately consumed him. All of his instincts told him to fight. Despite the other boy's warning from only minutes before, Jacques scrambled for his freedom, all legs, arms, and teeth going for anything.

To his surprise, Gregory let him go. Jacques paused for a millisecond to find his escape route but was instead met with four seamless white walls. A low chuckle beat his joy down.

"Where do you think you're going to go, hmmm?" Gregory said. "There is nowhere for you but this white room, my friend. Get used to it. Quickly."

Gregory marched over to Jacques and grabbed a hold of his left wrist. He dragged the frightened boy to his chair of doom and strapped him in with two-inch-wide leather straps around each ankle, wrist, and around his throat.

And that was the beginning of Jacques Dubois life as a test subject in the lab of Gregory Kempe.

18

"Wait, what?" Ashley said, more than a little gobsmacked. "Malaceia had you kidnapped from your family?"

Jacques nodded. "Every single wolf that has ever served alongside the Kempe family is or has been a shifter trapped in his wolf body. We've all been caught by unsuspecting humans being paid off by the organisation, and then shoved in Gregory's sick little lab, stuck with needles, cut with knives, and forced to hunt at their sides. Before Gregory, the witches would keep them as their shift animal with magick."

"Forced to hunt at their sides? How are you forced? You're not exactly kept on a leash, are you?"

Jacques smiled. "No. But the microchip we have in our neck ensures our good behaviour. They're tracking devices that also deliver a nasty little zap if we ever misbehave. Psychological fear worked before the microchips. When you've endured enough years of mental abuse and told that your family is in danger, believe me, no amount of wide-open space will make you even debate running. But then Katana happened, and my resulting behaviour brought about the introduction of the microchips."

Ashley frowned. "Go on."

"I hadn't been captured long—maybe three months max. Gregory had been acting strange the day before and when hours had passed and not one of us had been dragged out of our pitiful, gloomy cages, we knew something was up. A few of us, myself included, had turned on our last shift, and were struggling to turn back. This delightful little giggle sounded from the room next door, followed by 'Daddy?'. Then, just like an angel walking into the pits of hell, in walked Katana, holding the rock salt necklace she still has to this day as a light. She skipped into our room, giggling and looking for her father. When the light from her necklace lit up the end of the room and all of us, she stopped and gasped. Then, she rushed forwards and undid all of our cages. Dylan did nothing but sit in his cage, even though the door was swinging wide open. He'd given up all hope of ever going home."

"So how did you get out?"

"She told us all to follow her and motioned us towards the black chair that we all knew so well. A few of the boys became suspicious and turned back to their cages, thinking it was just a sick test or some sort of new experiment Gregory had planned."

Ashley raised an eyebrow. "Was it?"

"No, thankfully. But we'd all learned that Gregory is capable of anything. Only four of us followed her to that chair."

"Then what happened?"

"Just as fits with Gregory's twisted humour, Katana pressed a small button on the side of the chair. The damn thing moved to the side and beneath it opened a doorway. She skipped down the stairs, led us across an empty basement and then up another flight of stairs. When we reached the door at the top of these stairs, it opened out into Malaceia's office. She pointed to the open window and watched us all run for our freedom. I was nearly two miles away when I heard Malaceia's shout of fury at her. He was livid."

Ashley laughed. "Jeeze, I bet he nearly exploded from the anger."

"I nearly turned back to help her, but I'm a selfish coward and I kept running. I ran, and I ran, and I ran. I stopped only for water and the briefest of rests before I picked up the pace again. Eventually, I found myself on the borders of Mongolia, China, and Russia. A tribe of natives were going to kill me until I gave in and spoke to them. They were so shocked by a talking wolf, they almost fainted. It turned out they were a pack of shifters themselves—tiger shifters."

Ashley gasped. "No. Don't tell me the same pack that was ripped apart by civil war?"

Jacques winced and nodded. "I don't know how he did it but Malaceia found me. It took him several months, but he damn well found me."

"What did he do?"

"He put a knife to my throat and said I could either go home with him or die."

Ashley's mouth dropped open. "What did you do?"

"I chose die."

"What? Seriously?"

Jacques nodded. "He didn't like it and couldn't go through with killing me. Instead, he grabbed a hold of the pregnant woman whose cabin I was staying in. He slit her belly wide open and then slit her throat."

Ashley gasped. "No. He really did that?"

Jacques nodded. "That's when I knew I was already beaten. It was just a matter of casualties in the meantime. When he put his knife to the heart of a four-year-old girl, I knew I had to come home."

"What a callous bastard. And Katana doesn't know?"

Jacques shook his head.

"What happened with the pack? What did they do?"

Jacques barked with laughter. "The slimy bastard had stuck them all with a sedative whilst we were sleeping—they couldn't shift. By the time he'd killed the pregnant woman, they were only just getting the use of their limbs back. The war between them happened after we were long gone."

"Do you know what the war was about?"

"I don't know for sure, but I can hazard a guess. Some of the pack were ok with me and my situation. They wanted to help me. Others were

121

hesitant about taking me in; they foresaw the trouble I'd bring to their doorstep. Guess they were right."

"My God." Ashley swallowed the lump in his throat. "I'm astounded. I knew Malaceia had some shady depths, but that's just uncalled for."

"Welcome to the truth of Malaceia Kempe."

"What happened when you got back?"

"I hit the jackpot—Katana's mum, Shania, saw me and said instantly I was to be Katana's partner. Malaceia hated it. His face looked like he'd just swallowed a bunch of lemons. But, considering her status and power in the Amethyst Coven, who was he to deny her? Katana had unknowingly just saved my life. Ever since that day, I've made it my mission to protect her from the truth of her wicked father and to put my life before hers."

"So what's changed?"

"I snuck down into the basement a few weeks back—whilst Gregory was testing on you guys."

"I thought I sensed something. I thought I was going mad though."

Jacques nodded. "No, you weren't going mad. It was me. When I realised what he was doing, I knew something had to be done. Whether it's Gregory on his own or Malaceia at his side too, they both need bringing down. I only know one person tenacious enough to do such a thing."

Ashley sighed. "Katana."

Jacques nodded. "Irony at its best, isn't it? She saves my life—twice if you count the fact she allowed me to escape, then I repay her by destroying her entire world. What more could a girl want?"

"Shit, man. I really don't know what to say. If I can help in any way, I'll be glad to." Ashley ran a hand through his hair and let out a long breath. "So if we manage to reverse the shift on you, what about the others?"

"Well, I guess they need to be given the option at least, don't they?"

"Have you considered the fact that to turn you back might be permanent? As in, you'd be stuck as a human not being able to shift into a wolf?"

Jacques laughed. "I think it's safe to say I've had a lifetime's worth of being a wolf. It really wouldn't make any difference to me if I couldn't turn into a wolf ever again."

Ashley leaned forwards, his eyes full of concern. "I just want you to be certain you've thought of every possible way this could go wrong before I start poking at possible avenues."

Jacques nodded. "I've thought about this every day since the day I realised I was stuck like this. I'm not going to beg you, but if there is a route you can explore, I would appreciate it."

"Consider it done." Ashley stood up and squared his shoulders. "I'll be going straight to the source, just so you know. Nothing better than straight from the horse's mouth, hey?"

Jacques nodded and stood up. "I'm sure I don't need to re-iterate this, but not a word to Katana?"

"You do realise we could both end up losing her?"

"Sometimes a great sacrifice is needed for the greater good."

19

Katana woke from a deep sleep by the incessant ringing of her mobile phone.

When it rang off and then shrieked straight back into life, she groaned and rolled over. Grappling her fingers through the air, she found the bedside table and the source of her annoyance.

She blinked her eyes open to see **ERICA** flashing on the screen. Immediately, her brain sprung into being wide awake.

"Hey," she said, sitting up and wiping the sleep from her eyes.

"Hey chick," Erica replied. "Sorry to call you so early but I've got a shield grading this morning at eight and I still haven't ironed my uniform."

Katana smiled. Typical Erica to leave everything until the last minute—including an official assessment of her own magickal powers that could effectively decide if she's worthy to work for The Red Riding Hoods or not. "Don't worry about me. You need to worry about your own stuff first."

"No," Erica said, dropping her voice to a whisper. "I had to call you. I've re-routed your tracking device but there's a problem."

Katana groaned. "No. No problems, Erica. Please."

"You haven't got another case, honey. Your dad wanted you back home."

Katana's heart stopped and did a backflip. She'd never bothered to open Sophia's email after calling Erica. "No. Oh, God."

"It's ok—for now. I've put a pre-recorded route into the system and hooked your tracking device to it. It basically looks like you're on your way home. All the drivers are booked out on other jobs, so I've been in on Sophia's name and put a note on your profile saying you were happy to travel back on your own arrangements. You've got a couple of days, max, before questions start being asked."

"Marvellous. What the hell am I supposed to do in a couple of days? I need evidence, proof, something to back up what I've found out. Tell me you've got something from Dad's computer?"

Erica sighed. "I'm struggling, chick. Everything is so locked down with encryption, false links, and scattered files, it's like trying to find a trail of breadcrumbs in a bakery."

Katana's heart sank to her feet. This was not what she wanted to hear. "No." She let out a shout of frustration. "This sounds so stupid but I kinda expected you to download everything on a USB stick, give it to me, and ta-dah, job done."

"I know. That's what I expected too. I should have known better. I'm sorry, I'll keep trying." Erica sighed. "There's something else though.

The main attack map—you know the one that pings up on the start-up screen—it was flooded with red dots this morning. Whatever the hell is going on, werewolf attacks have literally increased ten-fold."

Katana jumped out of bed and began scrabbling around for her clothes. "I need you to link me to those attacks. Any attacks that have happened in the past forty-eight hours, can you please ping them straight through to my phone with all the relevant details?"

"Sure, that's easy enough. What the hell is going on?"

"Well, to put it simply, Gregory has created around eighty hybrids and infected them all with a virus."

"A virus?"

"Yes. An 'easy delivery' method that will ensure the continued numbers of werewolves."

A gasp sounded down the line. "Are you kidding? Oh my God."

"He's let twelve of them loose at the moment, but it's only a matter of time until he releases the rest. This is now a good old-fashioned case of one bite and the person will either turn or die."

"Is there anything I can do?"

"Yes. Pass your bloody shield exam."

The girls laughed, each of them ignoring the uneasy undercurrent. They said their goodbyes, both of them wondering just how the hell their worlds were about to change.

20

Katana yanked open her bedroom door and rushed downstairs. Words and thoughts tumbled through her mind; she didn't know what to announce first.

When an empty house stared back at her, dread settled in her stomach.

Oh no. Have they been fighting?

She rushed to the front door and pulled it open. Jacques padded lazily towards her with a dead bird hanging from his mouth. Ashley stood near the end of the paddock, on the phone, seemingly engaged in a rather animated conversation with someone judging from his erratic arm movements.

Breathing a sigh of relief, Katana narrowed her eyes on Jacques. "Have you calmed down since last night?"

Jacques dropped the bird onto the concrete area outside the front door. The clatter from its beak hitting the floor made Katana jump. He then laid down next to his kill, grabbed hold of it with his mouth, and dragged it back to him, settling it between his front paws.

He bit down on the bird's head, the crunch of its skull being crushed sending a shiver down Katana's spine. Pointedly ignoring her, Jacques continued to chomp and munch on his breakfast.

"I'll take that as a no then, shall I?"

Turning on her heels and heading back inside, Katana slammed her way around the kitchen, looking for something to eat, of which, there was nothing.

Just as she picked up a heavy saucepan, intending to hurl it across the room to alleviate some stress, Ashley waltzed back indoors, his green eyes glittering and a big smile on his face.

"Good morning," he said. "Did you sleep well?"

Katana lowered her stress relieving object and glared at him. "Fantastic. You?"

"Didn't sleep a wink. Hungry?" He motioned towards the saucepan. "Hate to tell you this but there's no food left in the cupboards."

"I know." Katana fixed him a deadpan stare. Her nostrils flared as her blue eyes oozed contempt. "I wonder why."

"Alright, chill out. We'll go and get some supplies now. Is that ok?"

"No," she said, snorting. "The point is I shouldn't have to get supplies because the supplies should bloody well be in here!"

"Whoa. Someone needs a chill pill."

Katana couldn't help herself. Before she knew what she was doing, the saucepan was flying through the air, aimed at Ashley.

For all his lab sufferings were worth, Ashley was blessed with quick reflexes. He dodged to the side and watched the saucepan sail straight through the space that would have been the middle of his face.

"Nice aim," he said, chuckling.

"Shame it wasn't a knife," Katana replied. "You might not have dodged a lighter object."

Ashley walked towards her, keeping his eyes locked on hers. "Now that's not a nice thing to say to your soul-mate, is it? Do I need to kiss you again to calm you down?"

"Ha! Just you try it, matey. I dare you."

Backed up against the small sink with a wall to her right and a very small gap to her left before the kitchen surface came around in its L shape, Katana found herself trapped as Ashley strode towards her.

He stopped one stride out and flashed her a smile. "You're pretty when you're angry. Anyone ever told you that?"

Katana knew he was provoking her, wanting a reaction. It was just a matter of ignoring it, not rising to the occasion. After a few seconds of chewing on some questionable words, she replied, "You should see me when I'm murderous then."

Ashley laughed and held his hand out to her. "Come on," he said, motioning towards the door with his head. "Let's go get stocked up."

"No. We're going hunting for your freaky phoenix siblings. I'll have the first target in the next few minutes."

"Are you forgetting this one that we still have to kill?"

Katana frowned, not understanding. Then, her brain kicked into gear, reminding her that the werewolf she'd killed had come back to life. It seemed like a whole other lifetime ago. "But we don't know what kills you freaks," she said, flicking a hand towards Ashley. "Have you got any way of knowing when he'll release the others?"

"Unfortunately, our shared werewolf DNA doesn't provide a psychic link to one another."

"All you had to say was no."

"No, I have no way of knowing when he'll release the others."

"Any clues whatsoever as to how to kill you phoenix freaks?"

Ashley started laughing. "Do you really think with your current hostile attitude that I'm going to even give you so much as an inkling as to what could kill me?"

"You really do love yourself, don't you?"

"I beg your pardon?"

Katana shrugged her shoulders. "Well, you seem to make everything about you. It's really not attractive you know, a lack of modesty."

Ashley narrowed his eyes. "Alright. Yes, I have a suspicion of one method. It involves water and whole lot of it."

"Ok. Care to explain?"

"Gregory tried drowning us in both human and werewolf form, but he never drowned us whilst we were in between. I think that's the key."

Katana frowned. "You mean when the flames start but before the phoenix rises?"

He nodded. "All you'd need to do is submerge us in water. I think."

"Ok, it sounds plausible but at that point, there's no body—you're just a pile of ash."

Ashley shrugged his shoulders. "Well that's simple enough. We'd simply let them burn to a pile of ash and then dump the ash in the sea or a lake or a river. Job done."

"Oh," Katana said, her voice laced in sarcasm. "Simples. Just like that. Hell, we might even get the other eleven of you all in one day." Struggling to keep a lid on her temper any longer, Katana exploded. "You're a fucking idiot. Get out of my way."

Ashley stepped to the side and allowed her to stomp past. He watched with a high degree of amusement as she marched outside, muttering and mumbling to herself. When he heard a scuffle followed by a loud thump a few seconds later, he dared to look out the door.

Katana was sprawled across the ground, face first, her laces from her long riding boots trailing in the dirt. She'd obviously forgotten to tie them up and had tripped over them. She stood up, glanced behind her at Ashley and said, "Not a fucking word."

21

By the time the fractured trio finally made it into the woodland, dawn had well and truly broken.

As normal, Jacques padded ahead, nose to the floor, trying to pick up a scent.

"Can you turn at will?" Katana said, glancing down at Ashley.

"Not technically speaking."

"What do you mean?"

"Well, we have some control. Gregory keyed the virus into the human emotions though. With werewolves, the virus breaks through and turns when they give in to lust."

"Lust?"

Ashley nodded. "Yes. You do know what lust is?"

Katana shot him a withering glance. "Yes, Ashley. My question was more of a how does it work type of thing."

"Ok. Here's how it worked with me. I have a real weakness for sour cherries—you know, the fizzy flavoured sweets?"

Katana nodded.

"Gregory bought a bag of them and told me they were mine. Then he left them outside my cage, just out of reach. For three days that damn orange bag sat an inch away from my fingertips.

There were times when I was drooling, you know. I'm not ashamed to admit it."

Katana giggled, imagining the scenario in her mind.

"He gave me the bag on the fourth day but warned me if I ate one, that would be the end of me. I craved after those damn sweets for another two days before I finally gave in. As soon as I decided I was having a sweet, that was it—I turned. I'd given in to my lust mentally and that's what allowed the virus to break through. It was my weakness."

"So it's ok whilst you're fighting it then? It's just when you give in?"

"Yes. It's always there, lingering beneath the surface, just waiting to force its way through."

Katana giggled. "Like the Hulk?"

Ashley looked up at her, confused. "What?"

"His secret for controlling his alter ego is he's always angry, despite the loss of control of his emotions being the trigger. So your secret is the same? That you're always…wanting something? Always lusting?"

Ashley looked straight ahead, seeming to ponder over her question. "I guess it is, yes."

"So what happens when you stop lusting instead of giving in?"

"I turn."

"So either way you're screwed then really?"

"Yeah, pretty much," he said, chuckling.

Realising she had a first-class opportunity to interview a werewolf here, Katana carried on probing. "What does it feel like? When you turn?

Do you know what you're doing or is it a blind rage that you forget when you wake?"

Ashley pursed his lips, then laughed. "You know when you have a really big spot? It's not quite ready to burst but it damn well hurts in the meantime?"

Giggling, Katana nodded.

"It feels like that. It's like a deep, burning ache that runs right through your body and into your bones. When you turn, it's like you're a spectator in your own body. You can hear things and see things, but you have absolutely no control over anything. It's like you're watching your body being used as a puppet. It's quite traumatic because the overwhelming sensation of being powerless and helpless is just...I can't describe it. I think a lot of people play the amnesia card because the brain either does genuinely block it out, or they just don't want to think about it."

"What does it feel like when you wake up?"

"You have that horrible, stomach full of dread feeling like when you wake from a nightmare. More often than not, you're covered in blood, sweat, and gasping for breath."

Katana shivered, suddenly realising that the werewolves she'd been slaying were people—actual human beings trapped inside an uncontrollable beast.

"When did you last turn?"

"When I was in the lab, so don't worry, I think you're safe." Ashley laughed.

Katana fixed him a blank stare. "You only came out of the lab a few days ago."

"When you're turning twenty times a day, a few days is a long time."

"Twenty times a day?"

Ashley nodded. "Gregory was desperate to find a way to make us die."

Katana fell silent. She couldn't believe the depths of the depravity her family, her own flesh and blood, were inflicting on other people. This wasn't right. None of this was. Something needed sorting, and soon.

But first, there was the small problem of eleven other immortal hybrid werewolves running rife, infecting any human they came across with the werewolf virus.

"But how was he making you turn so much? Surely, if anything, you were lusting after being free?"

"Oh yes," he said, nodding. "But that's nothing a little injection won't fix." He lifted the sleeve of his t-shirt, showing off his ripped muscles to Katana. His entire upper arm was pepper-marked with dots—needle injection sites. "My left side is just as bad."

Katana gasped. "My goodness. You look like…" her cheeks flushed pink as she said her next words "…a junkie that's been hitting up."

"Thanks." Ashley laughed. "I'm sure the feelings they get from their injections are much more desirable than what we got from these."

Katana gave him a smile tinged with sadness. "I'm so sorry you had to live through that. How were the others? Like, what were they like as people?"

Ashley shrugged his shoulders. "Some were ok. Some not so much. Just like regular people, I guess."

"Did they all have supernatural foundations—like you being a witch?"

He shook his head. "No. Some were regular people. He wanted to see the difference between regular humans and how it affected them, and then of course us supernaturals and how it affected us. That werewolf you killed? That's the human version of me."

"What other basics were used? Apart from the human and the witch DNA?"

"They were it. I did hear him talk about trialling shifter DNA but as far as I know, that's for a different experiment."

"So there's six of you witch based phoenixes and six human based phoenixes?"

Ashley nodded. "But each of us is slightly different. The other witch-based phoenixes like me are a little…peculiar. One in particular. I think our magick affected us all in different ways when we turned."

"How so?"

"Well, this one guy, his name was Stefan Lear, he harboured such a deep thirst for the macabre, spilling blood, killing—it literally drove him mad. He didn't care how many times a day Gregory stuck him with a needle, all he wanted was to rip things apart. He very nearly got a hold of

Gregory one day. Shame the slimy bastard had a taser in his pocket."

"But isn't that the basics of a werewolf anyway? To want to rip things apart?"

"To a degree, yes. But this was like on a whole new level. Think of crimes of passion as being what drives a werewolf—the heat of the moment, the loss of control—it's just a rampage of unbridled emotions. Then, think of a serial killer. Someone to the depths of Bundy or Dahmer. They cause just as much carnage but it's all that more chilling because it's been planned. They worked stuff out before they did it."

"And that's what this guy, Stefan, did?"

Ashley nodded. "I can guarantee you he won't be running wild through the streets biting anyone he comes across. He'll be sat alone somewhere, in the quiet, working out the best strategy for the maximum effect."

A shiver ran down Katana's spine, so violent she noticeably shivered in the saddle. "That's disturbing. Were there any others like him?"

Ashley looked up at her, hesitated for the briefest of seconds, and then nodded.

"Do you know who it is we're hunting up here?"

"Yes. It's him—Stefan"

Goosebumps raised all over Katana's body. "Are you telling me that the psycho who plots and plans is still out here and probably watching us right now?"

"Yeah…when I rugby-tackled you earlier, it was because I'd seen him just behind Jacques. I thought he was going to make his move."

"So you dove at me and gave me concussion?"

Ashley laughed. "Hey, I was trying to save your life."

Katana laughed. "I guess you can be forgiven for that."

Katana's phone pinged, breaking the conversation. Knowing that would be Erica's meddling linking her with the latest cases, she pulled her phone from her pocket.

With her heart in her mouth, she opened her phone screen and clicked on the red cape app icon for her family's business system. A black background supported an outline of Europe in bright blue. Hundreds of little dots spanned across the map; green for assigned cases, red for new cases, and white for recently solved.

Usually, at any one point in time, there would be no more than a hundred dots across the great expanse, all roughly even in their coloured dots.

This time, there were over one hundred red dots—and that was just in England.

22

Seeing the unfolding nightmare right in front of her eyes, Katana pulled Altair to a halt and called Jacques to come back to her.

"Right. Time for us to get practical. Erica called me this morning—Dad didn't have a new case for me, he wanted me home. As it stands, we have two days, max, before questions start being asked. I'm fully expecting him to call me in the meantime. Erica said all the drivers are on jobs so it was perfect for making me look like I'm making my own way home—hence the timeframe." Katana passed her phone over to Ashley. "Those red dots are new cases. We have a big problem."

Before either Ashley or Jacques could respond, another ping chimed through the air. Ashley gasped. "There's more red dots."

Jacques coughed and glared at Ashley. "You're obviously forgetting I'm not bi-pedal."

Ashley apologised before squatting down and sharing the unfolding crisis with him. Jacques scrutinised the screen and sighed. "Any suggestions? There must be a way to kill them all without having to chase down each individual one?"

"What do you mean?" Ashley said. "Like with vampires and their sires? Kill the sire and you kill the line?"

"Yes. This is science, and Gregory is Gregory. He'd have put a contingency plan in place in case of an instance like this."

"Why would he?" Katana said. "He's trying to infect the entire world but what he's not thought about is the people who pay us will also end up werewolves at some point."

Ashley gasped. "No. No, he's not that stupid—he'd have thought about that." He stood up and handed Katana her phone back. "These attacks won't be random—he'll have keyed in specifics somewhere. The problem is figuring out what."

"How the hell are we supposed to do that?

"Well, I know what he wanted us phoenix hybrids to do."

Katana raised her eyebrows. "Well don't keep the details to yourself."

"He wanted the phoenix hybrids to harvest organs." He looked down at the floor as he shuffled from foot to foot. "From children."

Katana glared at him with such bitterness, she could have soured milk. "This is your last chance to tell us if that was you that killed the girl."

"No," he said, throwing his hands up in the air in exasperation. "I promise you, it wasn't me. The wolf you killed is the wolf responsible, but of course, he's not dead and we have nothing but a theory on how to kill him."

"Right," Jacques said, stretching his limbs out. "Then let's focus on catching one and testing the theory. If it works, we're golden."

Katana frowned. "But that's still eleven werewolves we've got to hunt down—in less than two days. With the travelling, let alone the hunting, it's not physically viable. It's impossible. We'll struggle to catch one a day."

"Unless we split up?" Ashley said. "If we all take one each, that's three a day we can handle."

"No." Katana's sharp voice sent a jolt right through Ashley. "I don't hunt without Jacques, and he doesn't hunt without me."

Ashley grimaced. "He's a wolf, Katana. I think he can handle himself. We all know you're fine with your butchery swords and everything." He waved a hand at her katana sword.

"I said no."

"You need to break the apron strings one—"

"I SAID NO."

Silence hung in the air. Katana glared at Ashley as he glared back at her. Jacques, feeling very much like the elephant in the room, stared at the floor, speechless for once.

"So what about going back to the lab?" Jacques said, after a few tense minutes. "Figuring out if we can kill the entire line by killing one."

"But then that'll kill Ashley too," Katana said. Her phone pinged again with more new case alerts. She didn't even bother looking at it.

Jacques, whilst ignoring her comment about Ashley, had an epiphany. A jigsaw puzzle clicked into place. "The microchips—like what us wolves have. He'd have put trackers in them. That's our in—that's how we do it. You'll need Erica."

"No," Katana said, shaking her head. "She won't do it. She'll feel too guilty about helping to kill them, even if it is just giving us their locations." Katana remembered Ashley's words about what it felt like to turn. "And quite frankly, so would I."

Jacques gasped. "Since when have you had a conscience about killing werewolves?"

"Since I realised they are people inside those bodies, Jacques. Not everyone gets amnesia."

"How do you know?"

"Tell him, Ashley. Tell him what it's like when you turn."

"Are you kidding me?" Jacques said, snorting in disgust. "For all we know, K, he's a part of this whole conspiracy and wanting his damn freaky counterparts running loose. Maybe he wants you to sympathise with them so in the meantime, they can deliver their virus whilst you're playing tug of war with your heart and your head."

"Jacques!"

"No, Katana." He shook his head. "You're not thinking clearly. You need to keep your defences up and be suspicious of anything and everyone until you know better."

"Well, that means you're on the list as well then."

Jacques frowned. "How do you figure that? How am I a threat or a part of this sinister plan your family is cooking up?"

"I'm not saying that, Jacques. You said to be suspicious of anything and everyone until I know better. Well, until yesterday, I never would have considered the fact you would lie to me, but hey, life's a bitch."

Katana kicked Altair forwards into a canter and urged him over the wild landscape.

"Katana!" Jacques called after her.

She ignored him.

Jacques bolted after her, worried about what she was thinking and where she might be going. "Katana, stop!"

Altair's chestnut hindquarters continued to bounce into the distance.

Jacques stopped, lifted his muzzle, closed his eyes, and howled. The long drawn out cry echoed around the quiet moorland.

Birds fell silent. Insects stopped buzzing. Even Ashley held his breath.

The sad bay emanating from the white wolf's chest coated everything in such despondent emotion, the entire place felt like it had fallen into a deep depression.

When Jacques finished, he looked in the direction of which Katana had gone, his dark eyes bright and hopeful. His acute hearing picked up the faint sound of twigs snapping and leaves rustling. Then, the steady vibration of something approaching pounded through the earth, sending tingles right up through his legs.

Seconds later, Altair's chestnut head appeared, his ears pricked forwards, his nostrils flared wide, and his legs moving so fast they were almost a blur.

As he neared, Jacques could see his head held high and his whiskey coloured eyes were gleaming with joy. Anyone could see that the horse lived for speed.

On top of his slim back sat a red-faced Katana, shouting at her steed to stop, but her shouts were fruitless wastes of breath.

Altair locked onto his target—Jacques—and lowered his head as he pushed for a final spurt of speed.

Twenty feet out, he shifted all of his weight onto his haunches and jammed on the brakes. Dirt, leaves, moss, and twigs all spun up into a cloud either side of him as he skidded across the earthy floor.

Coming to a stop right in front of Jacques, Altair's left foreleg nudged Jacques' ribs. The gelding lowered his head and snuffled through Jacques fur, nuzzling him with affection.

Katana jumped down and glared at Jacques with her hands on her hips. "What the hell was that?"

"That was my emergency call."

Katana lifted her eyebrows. Shock settled across her features. "Oh. Something else you kept from me." She snorted and turned to Altair's side. She unhooked her katana sword and marched past Jacques, leaving Altair with him, and giving her wolf an evil stare. "I don't even know why I'm surprised."

As she turned her attention back to the way she was walking, she bumped into a solid body. "What do you want?" she said, rolling her eyes at Ashley.

"You're being unreasonable. Whatever is going on with you two, and us two, needs to be put aside whilst we deal with the job in hand. We need to control the hybrids and control their attacks."

"And how do you suggest we do that?"

"Well, the way I see it, we've got two options—we draw them somewhere, bottleneck them, and slaughter them, or we ask for help."

"From who?"

Ashley shrugged his shoulders. "I could ask Lenore and Arald."

Katana's gut twisted into a tight knot. It had been so long since she'd seen her uncle Arald. The last time she'd seen him, he'd been bleeding from a fight with her father. The idea of reaching out to him with something as huge as this didn't sit well with her.

"No," she said, shaking her head. "I don't want to go to uncle Arald. I don't know the details of what caused him to abandon the family to risk involving him. If we involve him, his motives may be more than helping the situation."

Ashley frowned. "What do you mean?"

"Well he and my father had a huge fight. That was the last time they spoke. If I suddenly call him up and say 'hey, there's a chance my dad might be up to no good,' what do you think he's going to do? He's going to want revenge."

"You don't know your uncle very well."

Katana narrowed her eyes. "It's a risk I'm not taking. There's enough going on without involving a revenge driven man."

Ashley shrugged his shoulders. "Like I said, you really don't know—"

"Ashley, if you say that once more I'm going to kill you. Again." When his mouth closed, Katana nodded. "Good. Before we decide who to go to for help, we need to figure out what our aim is here."

"What do you mean?" Jacques said.

"Well from the enormity of what's been revealed so far, there's enough to bring down the entire organisation and put my family in prison for a very long time. Is that something we really want?"

"They've committed a terrible crime, K," Jacques replied. "They need to answer for it."

Katana closed her eyes and sighed. "This is my family, Jacques," she said, opening her eyes again. "Without them, I'll have nothing."

Jacques looked at her, his brown eyes full of sympathy but edged with a tone of 'I told you so.'

"This is what you meant, isn't it? When you told me if I pick at this I'll end up alone?"

The wolf nodded. "I'm sorry, Katana, I really am."

"It's not your fault, Jacques. You're a victim in all of this."

Ashley cleared his throat. "Can I offer a point of view maybe?"

"Go on," Katana replied.

"Say you do nothing. Say we leave this alone as it is. I go home, you go home, that's it. As the virus spreads, how are you going to feel?"

Katana pursed her lips and pondered over her answer for a good minute. "Well, I'll feel guilty, definitely. Guilty of the fact that I knew about it but did nothing to stop it."

"Ok. Is that something you could live with for the rest of your life?"

She shook her head. "No. Especially not as I'd have to be one of the ones going out hunting them down and killing them. It would mess with my head too much."

"Ok, so the first step is resolved. You know you have to do something about it."

Katana smiled at him. "Clever. Nicely done."

"If you keep this between the family, what will happen?"

"You mean if I confront my dad?"

Ashley nodded.

"I have absolutely no idea. Knowing Dad, he'll either do his best to convince me that it's for the 'greater good' or whatever or…" dawning realisation struck her at this moment "…he'll do nothing."

"So you risk being stuck with guilt again and also causing a rift in the family?"

"Yes, but there's also the flip side to this. Say I hand over my own flesh and blood to the Council, do you not think that's going to cause some internal conflict too? Either way, I'm going to be ridden with guilt and end up falling out with my family. It's a lose-lose situation."

"It all depends what you can live with better. Saving thousands of innocent people or saving your own family?"

Katana gave him a small smile and sighed. What the hell was she supposed to do?

23

After a trip into Dalmellington town to grab some supplies to re-stock the cupboards, Ashley and Katana arrived back at the hunting lodge.

Jacques was curled up in front of the log burner, fast asleep. Katana wanted to ask him about his story with her father but at the same time, she didn't want to stir any more ill feeling the poor guy must have towards her family.

"Have you had any more thoughts about what you're going to do?" Ashley asked her as he helped her put the shopping away.

"I don't think I have a choice, really. I have to take this to the top. Shut it down completely."

Ashley lifted an eyebrow and let out a low whistle. "That's a big move. Are you sure about that?"

"Either way, I've lost my family. If I leave it at confronting my dad and let him sort something out, how am I ever going to trust that he has actually done something? I'll never know if he's just taken it further underground and out of range of anyone but him and Gregory."

"Is that what you think he would do?"

"He's a survivor. He'll do whatever it takes to keep the business going—this alone has shown that. I just thought..." she sighed "...maybe there might still be a piece of emotion left in him somewhere."

"I hate to say it, but business is business. I wasn't lying when we first met—about being a hunter. That's what Lenore was training me for, and your uncle Arald."

Katana frowned. "Seriously?"

"Yes. I'd already been hunting covertly for nearly a decade before Gregory got his hands on me."

"How did Gregory get hold of you?"

Ashley opened his mouth to speak but Jacques ambled through from the living room. "Please tell me you got me something nice to eat?"

Katana grinned and reached inside a plain white bag. "Prime cut of steak." She unwrapped it and threw it to her friend. "Cost a fortune so you better enjoy it."

Jacques caught his lump of meat mid-air, the snap of his jaws cutting through the silence. He turned and trotted off, looking rather pleased with himself.

"What were we talking about?" she said, turning back to Ashley.

"Business being business," he replied. "The point I was making was that some of the creatures I hunted were human when I killed them. Money is money. After a while you stop seeing people and just see pound signs. It's just a name or a case number worth X amount. There's no emotion involved. Like I said, it's business. I do understand where Malaceia is coming from with it."

"That doesn't make it right though. I feel like this has been revealed to me for a reason and that reason is to do something about it."

"Ok, so if you go to the Council, what do you think they'll do?"

Katana shrugged her shoulders. "I don't know but once they're involved, things will be done by the books. Hell, by the time they're involved, Gregory may have even let the other hybrids loose by then."

"That's more than feasible. With the range of creatures there are, they may out-source to some unofficial hunters or even ask the other elite families first if they're interested in helping."

"But there's still people inside those creatures, Ashley. What if we can help them instead of kill them? Isn't the Council supposed to look out for the innocent civilians as well?"

Ashley scrubbed a hand over his face. "Look, I know you're all confused and overwhelmed but you're forgetting that the people that are in those bodies are gone—they don't have any control or any say over what happens to them. The part of them in there is so small, they'd feel nothing but relief at being killed, trust me."

"So if you were part of the hybrids that you're saying is going to be hunted and slaughtered, that's how you'd feel is it?"

He shrugged his shoulders. "Pretty much. There's two options—death or living a life through a keyhole being an audience to something using your body."

Katana sighed and pondered over her options. Whether it was her, Ashley, and Jacques that did it or the Council, these hybrids were going to die either way. However, what really mattered was the method of which it was executed.

Enticing them all to one point seemed like a good plan but to then engage in a mass slaughter? That didn't sit right with her.

Maybe she could talk to the Council before they decided on a mass execution method?

"Ok. The way I see it is the hybrids are going to die either way."

Ashley stared at her, silent.

"Be straight with me, Ashley. That's what's going to happen, isn't it?"

"Yes. Unfortunately."

"Right. The key thing is to prevent this stupid virus from being spread even more which means I need to get my arse in gear and get someone involved now."

"I agree."

As if divine intervention was proving a point, Katana's phone pinged with the distinctive note that meant it was her family's app letting her know there were more cases.

"I need to call the Council. However, if I do that, I won't get a chance to speak to my father beforehand."

"And that's what you want to do?"

She nodded. "I want to let him know, face to face, that I know what he's been doing. I need to see for myself what his reaction is. I also want to give him the option to stop it. Just for my own peace of mind."

"Ok, I understand that. This is affecting your life too, so you need to be comfortable with the way things go down. I get that."

"Which means not going directly to one of the Councillors."

Ashley frowned. "How else are you going to involve the Council?"

"NO!"

Jacques loud bark made both Ashley and Katana jump.

"Jacques, I don't have another choice."

"Yes, you do. Call Erica and get Bryn involved."

"Bryn isn't interested in Council business, Jacques. He'll just pass it straight onto his mother without thinking about it. I need someone who understands the legalities and is willing to flex them a little so I can deal with this my way first."

Ashley frowned. "Am I missing something here?"

"Ask her who she wants to contact," Jacques said. He stepped forward and growled. "It's ridiculous at best."

"Jacques, it's logical."

"You think his price will be logical?"

"Hold on," Ashley said, holding his arms out to his sides, keeping Katana and Jacques at bay, even though there was no risk of them getting any closer. "What's going on? Who do you want to call, Katana?"

"A contact of mine. He's a Councillor's son."

Ashley nodded his head. "That doesn't seem like a bad idea. What's the problem, Jacques?"

"The person she's going to contact has been trying to marry her since she started her periods at the age of twelve. Her father supports the arranged marriage."

Katana glared at her friend with such disdain, the hatred rolled off her in waves. "You're a dickhead. I really don't like you sometimes."

Ashley's jaw dropped wide open. "Just how many guys have I got to contend with?"

"Is that all you can think about?" she snapped at Ashley. "The answer is none because I'm not a damn fairground prize. The sooner you get that in your head, the better. And as for Jacques, it's not like I'm into bestiality. Get your head out of your arse."

"You can't call this guy," Ashley said, shaking his head. "Jacques is right."

"Why? Do you think I'm ignorant to what his price will be? What other option do I have?"

"Don't call him. Go home, confront your dad, and if he does nothing, then call the Council. Cut out the middle guy."

"Clearly you don't know my father. If I go home now and confront him, lay out his options or whatever, I'll never see daylight again."

Ashley laughed. "Are you saying he'll keep you prisoner?"

"I know he'll keep me prisoner. If it's just me on my own there's nothing stopping him from doing it. It took him five years longer than normal to put me in the field in the first place. If anyone asks questions, he'll simply tell them I had a bad first case and I'm back in training or something. It's not hard for him to keep secrets, as we all know."

"Then I'll come with you," Ashley replied. "And Jacques will be there too."

Katana tipped her head back and laughed. "Right. The released lab experiment who was sent on a mission to claim his soul-mate and the other lab experiment who has a microchip in his neck to zap him whenever he's naughty?"

"You're being a defeatist."

"I'm being realistic."

"You really think this is your only option?"

"I know it's my only option."

"Would the Council not give you protection?"

"After I tell them all this, why the hell would they allow me back home to 'offer' my dad a hypothetical chance to settle my own mind? The Council will look at things like a business, Ashley. I would have thought you of all people would have understood that."

"And you really need to offer him that chance for your own peace of mind that badly?"

"Yes, I do." Katana folded her arms over her chest and fixed Ashley with a death stare. "This is my life and my way of having to deal with it. If you don't like it, you know where the door is."

Ashley shook his head and looked at the floor. "Fine. Whatever. Do whatever you need to do."

Katana took her phone from her pocket and headed outside. She sneered at Ashley. "It's not like I needed your permission anyway."

24

"Katana," came the lazy Norfolk drawl of Tobias Bembridge. "What a surprise to hear from you. Does this mean you have reconsidered my proposal?"

Katana gave a weak smile before she answered. "Not so much. This is more business than personal."

"Well, technically speaking our marriage would be considered business, would it not?"

She couldn't help but laugh. "I guess so."

"My father is very keen to have you in the family. It would be a fantastic allegiance for both sides."

"I'm not going to say I don't agree, Tobias, because I do. I just...there's so much going on right now, being a battery hen and popping out kids isn't high on my agenda."

He laughed. His haughty, deep voice echoed down the phone and covered Katana in goosebumps. "So what is high enough on your agenda to warrant a phone call to me?"

"Well, it's a bit sensitive. Can you promise me this will be kept strictly between us?"

Silence was the only reply for several seconds. "Why do I not like the way you're saying that?"

"Because you're paranoid?"

He laughed. "Or because this should be going higher but I'm a by-line, I'm guessing?"

"How do you know me so well?" she said, laughing.

A light chuckle warmed Katana's heart. "I'm going to be a bastard, Katana. I'll help you, you know I will, but I can't partake in underhand, secretive things without a high reward."

Katana's heart sank. She knew this would happen. A small part of her had hoped he wouldn't do it, just to stick two fingers up to Jacques and Ashley. "I wondered if that would be the case."

"I'm sorry," Tobias replied. "But you must understand the complications I face this end by betraying my family—especially with my father having such a high position on the Council. One small slip from any of us and all of that comes crashing down around our ears."

"I get it, I do. I'm sorry to ask something like this of you, I really am, but you must understand I wouldn't be asking if I wasn't desperate."

More laughter. "What a way to make a guy feel special, Katana. Bravo."

"I'm sorry," she said, laughing. "You know what I mean. I wouldn't put you in such a position if it wasn't absolutely necessary."

"I know," he said, still lightly chuckling. "But that doesn't mean I don't want a high reward— something that will justify my actions to anyone and everyone."

Katana sighed. "You want me to agree to marry you."

"It seems you also know me very well."

Apparently so. Katana closed her eyes and sucked in a deep breath.

Marrying Tobias wouldn't be the worst fate she could possibly endure. He was a stereotypical male of her world in that he expected a woman to be a woman—Katana's kick ass attitude, martial arts training, and sword swinging days would be well and truly over. She'd be resigned to a life of being pregnant and barefoot in the kitchen. Easy—yes. Enjoyable—at times. What she wanted—no.

However, thousands of lives were at stake here and Katana knew without a doubt she had to do something; even if that meant giving up her own dogged determination to make it as a hunter.

"Ok," she said. "I'll do it. I accept your proposal on the basis that you keep the following information strictly private."

"Deal. Let's keep the phone lines clear. Where are you? I'll come and meet you."

Katana faltered, not expecting that at all. Meeting him face to face? Was he going to want to kiss…and more? "Um, I'm in Scotland so it's not overly practical to meet really."

"That's not a problem. I have my pilot's licence now. The chopper came back yesterday from its routine maintenance. I can be with you in a couple of hours."

Of course you can. Katana didn't know what to reply except to meekly agree to meet her new fiancé face to face.

C.J. Laurence

25

After detailing Tobias on exactly where she was, Katana put the phone down and let out a breath.

This was a life-changing week for her; her family were a bunch of lying crooks, her best friend wasn't a wolf but a shifter trapped in his animal body, she had a soul-mate who was a werewolf-phoenix hybrid who couldn't die, and she'd just agreed to marry the one person she never imagined herself with.

Now, she had to go and tell both Jacques and Ashley that she was now engaged and having a secret rendezvous with her new fiancé in a couple of hours. Marvellous. Beheading and burning werewolves was a walk in the park compared to this.

Heading back indoors, Katana plastered a smile on her face and cleared her throat. "Well, we have some good news. We have some help coming. He'll be here in a couple of hours."

"Right…" Ashley said, eyeing her with suspicion. "And did he have a price?"

"Don't," Jacques said. "Don't tell me. You stupid girl."

Katana closed her mouth. Guilt swamped her. She knew Jacques would be mad and he had every reason to be. The discussions they'd had in the past regarding Tobias Bembridge and their more or less arranged marriage had put both her and Jacques on the same level. All of her integrity, what she valued about herself, and what she valued from life, had just been given away in a simple phone call.

"You agreed to marry him?" Ashley said.

"You need to understand the stakes are high his end. His father is a Councillor for goodness sake. The Bembridge name has to be squeaky clean—unless it's worth his while."

"You've basically prostituted yourself out, Katana," Jacques said, curling his top lip back in disgust. "I thought I knew you better than that."

A sharp barb of pain lodged itself in Katana's heart. "Well, I guess we're both learning new things about each other this week, hmmm? I had no choice. We need his help."

"No, Katana. There's always a choice." Ashley shook his head and turned his back on her. "I thought you had more about you than that."

"Fuck you," she said, stomping around to face him. "How dare you speak to me like that. I'm sacrificing my life here to keep thousands of people safe."

Ashley threw his head back and laughed. Then, he started clapping. "Well, bravo. At least you'll die a martyr, hey? Marvellous Katana Kempe giving up on her childhood dreams of being an amazing female hunter just to give in and start popping out kids to save the humans. Wow. It's almost like you're Mother Theresa reincarnated."

Katana couldn't help herself. It was instinctual. She slapped Ashley so hard around the face, her palm was stinging before she'd even registered what she'd done.

Emerald green eyes flashed at her with fury. Then, he doubled over, crying out in pain.

"Ashley?" Katana said, running to his side. "Are you ok?"

He held his arms around his middle and shouted out in pain. "Get away," he said, his voice now a deep growl. "Get away from me."

"Ashle—"

He turned his head and looked at her. Emerald green eyes were now a chilling shade of yellow. His canines were thickening and lengthening and his skin began to take a dark hue to it as black hairs sprung to the surface.

"He's turning!" Jacques said. "Get Altair. We need to move."

"But we can't leave him," she said, still holding Ashley's forearm. Thick, coarse hair now covered her small fingers, it's density still growing by the second. "We can help him."

"No, we can't," Jacques said. "Don't you get it? He no longer finds you desirable, Katana. He's lost control."

Dawning reality hit Katana square in the face, leaving her with a stinging soul. *Ouch.* Ashley no longer lusted for her. Why did this seem to bother her?

"Katana!"

In a daze, she turned to Jacques, still processing what was going on.

"Get the horse and let's MOVE," he yelled.

As Ashley's body twisted into the fearsome form of a werewolf, Katana pulled her wakizashi from her right hip.

"I'm sorry," she said to Ashley, then cut his head clean off.

Jacques stared at her, open mouthed. "What the…?"

"I've just bought us twenty minutes. Now move."

Becoming increasingly concerned at the person Katana seemed to be turning into, Jacques didn't dare argue otherwise.

26

The pair galloped through across the open wilderness as if their very lives depended on it. To be quite honest, they did.

Katana wasn't sure if Ashley would come back as him or as a werewolf, but she wasn't prepared to wait around and find out. She'd bought her and Jacques between twenty and thirty minutes. All that mattered was what they did with those minutes.

She'd arranged with Tobias to meet at the top of Galloway Forest Park. His family owned some land around Dalcairney so landing his chopper there posed no issues.

When Jacques realised they were heading towards the north-eastern area of the park, he slowed their pace to a walk and questioned Katana.

"Where are we going?"

"To meet Tobias. We're not far away."

"Yes, but *where?*"

"Near Dalcairney Falls."

Jacques froze. His right front paw was still in mid-air, waiting to meet the ground with his next step. "You...no..." he shook his head "...I'm not going there. No."

Katana frowned. "What? Why?"

"Because it's not a nice place."

"You've been there?"

"I was born there."

Katana gasped. "What? But...but I thought you were caught as a pup somewhere near Nottingham?"

Jacques barked with laughter. "Ha! After everything you've learned this week, are you really still hanging onto the notion that anything you know is true?"

"But...well, you've never told me any different."

"Well, now I am. Dalcairney is where I was born, and I am not going back there."

"Why not?"

"Because that's where I was taken from, Katana. Ok? I don't want the bad memories. I don't need the bad memories."

"Tell me what happened."

"No."

"Jacques, please. I'm trying to be a good friend here. Talk to me. Let me in. Please?"

"If you want to be a good friend then worry about being the person I know you to be."

"What's that supposed to mean?"

"That you don't pimp yourself out like a hooker and marry some Council idiot to try and make yourself feel better. People die every day, all day, Katana. There's nothing you can do about it."

"But these ones I can do something about. I can help them."

"Really? What exactly are you going to do to help those lab experiments and an unstoppable virus?"

Katana opened her mouth to reply, but no words came to mind. He had a point. What exactly was she going to do? What exactly was she expecting Tobias to do?

"I don't know," she said, tears welling in her eyes at just the frustration of it all. "But what I do know is I at least have to try, Jacques. If I don't try to do something then I'm just as bad as my father." She sighed and dismounted. "Look, I don't know what happened to you. I'm sure you'll tell me when you're ready, but whatever you went through, don't you want to stop others from having to suffer the same fate?"

Jacques closed his eyes and growled in frustration. "To a degree, yes. But past a certain point, K, I'm feeling nothing but total selfishness. I've suffered long enough at the hands of your family and I want out."

"Will you stop saying that, please?"

"What?"

"'Your family'. It's like you're personally accusing me of doing this to you."

"Are they your family?"

"Yes, you know they are."

"Then I'm well within my rights to use that phrase. It's a fact. How you perceive what I say is entirely your issue, not mine."

Katana narrowed her eyes at him, surprised at how much hatred was filling her heart towards her closest friend. "It's times like now where I wish I'd partnered with Dylan or Calhoun instead. You're being a pompous arsehole, Jacques."

Jacques glared back at her. His dark eyes glazed over with a dull, empty stare and the heckles on his back raised. "You're being a bitch just for the sake of it. You know what—if you think a wimp like Dylan or Calhoun is a better match for you, then you go right on ahead and partner up with them. Leave everything as it is and follow your father blindly into oblivion."

"You know who's the wimp?" Katana leaned forwards and stabbed her index finger through the air at him. "You. You're being the wimp because you don't want to go back home and stir up old memories. Well, boo-hoo. Grow a pair and for the sake of the damn world, Jacques, put others first instead of yourself."

"Instead of myself? Are you kidding me? What part of my miserable life makes me put myself first?" He closed the gap between them both and snarled at her. "What part of being your servant puts myself first? What part of being jabbed with needles, cut open like a frog, and left alone in the dark hour after hour for years on end puts myself first? You think I like being like this? I hate it. Every second of every day, I hate my life. Not even being with you is enough of a reward for being stuck like this. Don't you get it? I have no free choice in my life. I can't even eat what I want to eat because I'm stuck like this. Don't you think I'm sick of eating birds and rabbits whilst watching you eat juicy burgers and delicious rice dishes? Don't you think I'd like to stretch my legs, my *human* legs, and have a shower or go on a rollercoaster? Or even just have the ability to tell someone I love them without being laughed at because I'm stuck as a wolf?"

Katana had no words. Her mouth was open, but nothing computed in her brain to usher words past her lips. Guilt and sympathy tangled together inside her. She stepped backwards until she found her back against Altair's solid body.

"Ok," she finally said. She mounted Altair and glanced down at Jacques. "If you don't want to go there, then don't."

With that, Katana pushed Altair on, not even bothering to look back at Jacques.

27

Every part of Jacques wanted to run after Katana. She was his everything.

In times of his greatest darkness, she'd appeared like a ray of golden sunshine, freeing him into the world. Even when he'd been forced back to the grim reality of his life, she'd been there—a bright, joyful beacon in his sad, sorrowful world.

He knew he wallowed in self-pity some days, but in his mind, he was more than justified in doing so.

The horrors he'd had to endure day after day before he was even allowed to be with Katana were unspeakable acts that still penetrated his dreams even all these years later.

Maybe he needed to cut his apron strings in order to be who he needed, and wanted, to be. Maybe the conversation he'd had with Ashley earlier that morning needed personally acting on, by Jacques himself, now.

Maybe this was his time.

As he watched Altair and Katana disappear into the distance, he knew she'd be safe. The horse would outrun any werewolf between now and when Tobias appeared, and when Tobias did appear, he'd have guns and gadgets galore to keep any attacks at bay.

Figuring this was his now or never moment, Jacques decided to go straight to the source personally. He would go see Lenore himself and see if there was a way for him to be human once more.

Maybe, maybe then he could save the world.

28

Malaceia logged onto his computer system, dreading what he was going to see.

Sure enough, as soon as the system loaded, bright red dots pinged up on his screen, each one chiming its existence so that a constant ear-piercing note was all that could be heard for nearly a minute.

Biting back a stream of curses, he looked through his list of active hunters, searching for Katana. When he saw her name at the bottom of the list, he clicked on it and waited for the screen to load with her tracking map.

A small flicker interrupted the screen before it loaded the location of her whereabouts. According to the map, Katana was near Carlisle. He scrolled the wheel on his mouse, wanting to zoom in on an exact location, but the system froze, then kicked him out.

Frowning, he reloaded his daughter's location page. As he waited for the map to reappear, he noticed a note from Sophia saying that Katana had agreed to make her own way home as all the drivers were out on other jobs. With the recent influx of cases, that was more than understandable.

He sighed and leaned back in his chair. Drumming his fingers on his desk, he picked up his phone and toyed with the idea of ringing Katana. He was surprised he hadn't heard from her already, giving him a load of abuse for telling her to come home instead of giving her a new case.

As he stared blankly at the screen, the date and time of Sophia's note burned into his retinas. Something niggled in the back of his mind, but he couldn't quite put his finger on what.

Giving up on the idea of calling Katana, because he knew he wouldn't be warmly received, he put his phone back down on his desk and clicked on the earliest case this release of Gregory's 'pets' had done.

Its bright red, rapidly blinking dot with an exclamation mark in the middle of it told him it was the oldest case. The system was alerting him to the fact it still hadn't been assigned to anyone.

Then, something clicked inside Malaceia's head.

The date and time of the case was after the note had been put on Katana's profile.

If the case came in after Katana had started her journey home, then how could all the drivers be out on jobs because of the influx? At the time the note was made, things were still 'normal.'

He pushed a button on the underneath of his desk and yelled, "Sophia!"

Seconds later, a middle-aged lady came flying through the door. A little chubby in places, she was rather unremarkable otherwise. The perfect epitome of a 'plain jane.' "Yes, Sir?"

"This note you left on Katana's account states she's travelling home because all the drivers were booked out on other jobs. The timings don't add up as to why though. The influx didn't happen for nearly an hour afterwards."

Sophia frowned. Her dark, bushy eyebrows, that she never plucked, furrowed together in a mono-brow. "But I haven't spoken to Katana for anything."

"You must have done—there's a note here with your name on it. It's time stamped to 6.13am."

"But I wasn't even on the system then. Not this morning. I was in A&E with Roger all night because he had a grumbling appendix."

Malaceia raised a brow. "Is he ok?"

The woman nodded, her shoulder-level brown hair bobbing up and down with her movement. "They're giving him surgery today."

"What are you doing here then? Go."

Sophia shook her head. "There's no point. They wouldn't even let me on the ward. I can't do anything until he's in recovery and been dismissed to the day ward. They're going to call me when he's out of surgery. I'll go then."

Malaceia gave her a sad smile. "Your loyalty to this family is astounding, Sophia. It doesn't go unnoticed."

The woman gave him a thin smile. "Is that all, Sir?"

"If you're confident this note wasn't left by your hand?"

"Definitely not, Sir."

"That's all." He nodded her dismissal.

When the door closed behind her, Malaceia leaned forwards and reached for his phone. Perhaps it was time to call his wife on official business.

29

Katana was vaguely surprised Jacques didn't follow her. Perhaps because it was always his duty, his job to be at her side, but also maybe because whenever they argued, and she stomped off, he always chased after her.

But not this time.

Things in her world were changing at a startling rate. She couldn't deny he hadn't warned her not to go down this road.

The situation unfolding around her was altering her perceptions on her life as she knew it, so it was only understandable that it would also alter her as a person. She was the person she was because of her environment. For that environment to then be suddenly shaken up and flipped upside down meant she could only change to suit.

What exactly that meant for her and Jacques, time would only tell. As her and Altair cantered towards the hill Tobias had given her directions to, her mind wandered back to Ashley. He should still be 'dead,' which gave her some comfort in the time lost because of her argument with Jacques.

Looking at her watch, she tried to ignore the discomfort when she realised she had over an hour before Tobias arrived.

Even though she wasn't at her rendezvous point yet, the thing that worried her was the fact that over an hour meant Ashley could be killed and re-born roughly three times in that time.

Fighting with werewolves was a physically demanding job. She wasn't sure if she had it in her to fight and kill another three times in the next hour.

Werewolves were fast, she knew that much. If they were homed in on a target, not even God himself could stop that creature from getting to what it wanted.

Then a thought popped to mind. Now that she'd killed him, would he return as a werewolf or would he return as a human?

If he returned as a human, she had nothing to worry about, but of course, with all of the mayhem currently going on, she'd not even had a thought to think about asking him such a question. Her knowledge in her new world was somewhat limited at best.

Hoping and praying he returned as a human, Katana kept Altair at his current speed and rhythm, estimating they would reach their destination at roughly the same time as Tobias.

ജ

As Katana and Altair approached the peak of the hill, she could hear the distinctive buzz of an aircraft. With each passing moment, the noise became more noticeable as that of a helicopter rather than a plane.

When a huge black chopper came into eyesight, she bit back a groan. This was supposed to be a discreet affair, not a show of 'look at me and how much money I have.'

Still, remembering her newly engaged status, she plastered a sickly-sweet smile on her face as she awaited the arrival of her new fiancé.

Waiting in a small copse of trees for the helicopter to land in the wide-open space, Katana refused to move until the blades had come to a complete stop. By this point, Tobias was already out of the aircraft and walking across the wild landscape towards her.

He was dressed casually, in dark denim jeans and a tight-fitting white t shirt. Short, dark cropped hair, dark brown eyes, and tanned skin, he wasn't uneasy on the eye.

Katana decided to stay on board Altair, feeling somewhat more in control and safer from on top of him. She pushed him out into a trot, not wanting to seem too eager to gallop towards her 'love.'

"Hello there," Tobias said, flashing her a big grin. "You're definitely a sight for tired eyes."

Katana smiled. She would happily admit he was a charmer, but perhaps it was that exact thing that put her off him. He was almost too charming. "Hi yourself. Good flight?"

"As good as can be." He looked back at his chopper and then back to Katana. "I brought back-up with me. I hope you don't mind?"

Katana reached him and pulled Altair to a stop. She couldn't help but giggle. "So long as they don't ask questions, that's fine."

Tobias raised an eyebrow. "Believe me, they know better. They point and shoot. That's all they're paid for."

"Sounds good to me."

The two looked at each other as an awkward silence stretched between them. They both then started laughing.

"So, are you going to dismount and tell me what this is all about?"

Katana looked him up and down and decided she felt easy enough around his friendly demeanour to risk being on the ground.

She jumped down and loosened off Altair's girth before taking up the slack in his reins and looping them around the horn on the front of her saddle.

"I don't know exactly what I'm expecting you to do," she said, walking a few feet away from Altair. "But I'm hoping you can help me in some way."

"Ok," he said. He reached out a hand, offering for her to take it. "Let's take a walk and talk."

Katana shook her head. "I'm not going too far from Altair and you won't want to stray too far from your men and your helicopter either."

Whilst Ashley had yet to reappear, Katana was rather on edge for his expected return.

"Ok. Fair enough." Tobias folded his arms over his chest and smiled. "Bring me up to speed."

Katana took a deep breath and indulged him in what had been going on.

30

"**S**o right at this minute, where does your father think you are?" Tobias asked. He held his chin between his thumb and index finger, striking a pensive pose.

"On my way back home. But I don't know how long Erica's meddling will fool him for. He's not a stupid man."

"By all accounts, no, he's not. But judging him on what you've so far revealed to me, he is actually incredibly stupid. He's letting his lust for money and power get in the way of anything else."

Katana nodded. "Do you have any ideas on how to stop the hybrids?"

"Yes. That's quite easy. After the scandal between your father and your wolf, the Preternatural Council passed a law that said any supernaturally tainted being had to have a microchip implanted."

"I know about the microchips. Jacques told me all the wolves have them. They're a tracking device like the hunters but also have a 'zap' to make them behave if necessary. What scandal? What are you talking about?"

Tobias smiled. "Your tracking device is completely different to these microchips. Your friend is mistaken though. Yes, they have a 'zap,' but they will also end their life at the press of a button."

Katana gasped. She remembered her father's threat before she headed out on this case—that Jacques would be 'gone' if anything happened to her. Whilst she hadn't thought too much about how he would kill her friend, she'd never expected him to have the power to do so at the press of a button.

"Do the wolves know that?"

"Yes. It's a legal requirement that they're made aware of the power the organisation has over them."

Great. Something else Jacques kept from me.

"Don't you know what happened between your father and Jacques?" Tobias said.

"Does the expression on my face look like I know?"

He laughed. "To cut a long story short, Jacques and three others escaped Gregory's lab. Does that jog any memories?"

Katana frowned. "No. Why, should it?"

"Well, considering you were the one who let them out, yes."

"But I've never been down in Gregory's lab, let alone interfered with whatever he does down there."

Tobias tipped his head back and laughed. "My dear, Katana, I fear your mother may have used her powerful position to influence your memories. Here is the story as I know it…"

Ten minutes later, Katana sat on the floor, dazed and stunned. Not only had she learned she'd set her friend free, she'd learned why Jacques didn't want to come back to Dalmellington, and that her father was a callous murderer with little care or respect for anyone but himself.

To add to that, her mother had washed over her memories of setting the wolf-shifters free, seemingly erasing all knowledge of what she'd seen in Gregory's lab.

"And there was me thinking I couldn't be shocked anymore," she said, covering her face with her hands.

"Well, after Jacques' little escapade, the Preternatural Council demanded that any supernatural being be implanted with a microchip. It would mean the family would have total control of them at any given point regardless of where they were in the world."

"In other words, if he ran again, they'd flick a switch and kill him."

Tobias nodded.

"But what makes you think that Gregory put these microchips in the hybrids?"

"Because any mad scientist, no matter how mad, will need a back-up plan to cover his arse in case things go wrong. He wouldn't have not done that."

"Ok, I'm not entirely sold on that theory but working on the basis that he has, how can we access the data when it's in his lab?"

A broad grin spread over Tobias's face. His blue eyes glinted with joy. "Because the microchips can only be sourced from one place—the Preternatural Council. Before they're shipped out, each one is logged and coded onto our internal system. We know the second they're implanted and become active because they're keyed into the supernatural cells."

Katana's eyes widened. "Whoa. But with all the wolves we have as hunting companions, how are you going to know who is a wolf and who is a hybrid experiment?"

Tobias shrugged his shoulders. "Two ways. A simple cross-reference of microchip locations to the recent influx of cases. Also, the microchips have to be individually named as soon as they're active or the Council will fine your family."

Katana grinned. Suddenly having allegiances in high places seemed to be paying off. She started to understand why her father had wanted this marriage to happen so badly. If she'd married Tobias four years ago, which is what everyone had wanted, then this current problem wouldn't currently be a problem.

She checked herself.

Of course it would. Her marrying into the Bembridge family wouldn't have stopped Gregory playing with the hybrids nor stopped him letting them loose in a bid to spread a virus around the world. The only difference would have been to her knowledge of her world. She would have known nothing of the sick, twisted activities being undertaken and would have never have been in a position, like now, to do something.

Everything happens for a reason.

185

A thought pinged to mind. "Can you access that data from your phone?" Katana asked.

Tobias frowned and pulled his phone from inside his jacket pocket. It was a huge phablet; one of the latest releases from the looks of it. "Yes, why?"

"You need to access it. Now. To get the location of them."

Tobias tapped on the screen, waking the phone from its sleep. He swiped, tapped, and dotted around on the screen for several pain-staking seconds. "Ok," he said, flicking across the screen. "It seems they're still in the UK." He frowned. "This is really peculiar. Is this normal werewolf behaviour?"

Katana looked over his shoulder. "What?"

"It looks like they're in couples or small groups...most are still around the Nottingham area. A couple are near Manchester..."

Katana's stomach flipped upside down. "No. That's not normal behaviour at all. Are you telling me they're working together like that?"

"Judging from the distance they've travelled already, yes. I'd have expected them to scatter like marbles from your house, but they haven't." He let out a long breath and looked back down at his phone "Oh, hang on."

Katana's veins filled with dread. The hairs on the back of her neck stood up.

Altair lifted his head from grazing, peering behind him into the treeline.

"It looks like there's one not far from here..." Tobias moved his fingers apart on the phablet screen, zooming in on his information "…shit, it's actually really not far from here…."

Altair snorted and bolted to Katana. Without even hesitating, Katana reached for her katana sword and unsheathed it. She peered into the dark edge of the trees.

"According to this," Tobias said, looking up at Katana with confusion spread over his face. "It's about two hundred metres inside the woods. That way." He pointed to the direction Katana was already facing.

"Can you deactivate it from there?"

"What, the chip?"

"Yes," Katana replied, scanning her eyes over the unmoving nature before her. She tightened Altair's girth, ready to mount.

"You do realise that's it—they cease to exist?"

Katana spared him a glance. "Are you telling me you've developed a conscience now?"

"I've always had a conscience, Katana. I really do think you have a skewed vision of me. I'm not a bad guy."

"Perhaps now isn't the time to discuss your credentials as a person, let alone as a partner."

Tobias nodded and fiddled with his phablet screen some more. "Right. Are you sure you want this done?"

"What's the name registered to the chip?"

"Subject number H7A2. Stefan Lear."

Katana gasped. She'd expected the name to be Ashley's. "What? No. You must be wrong?"

Tobias put the screen in front of her, showing her the information he had to hand. "I can only read what's in front of me."

"Press it!" she yelled. "Press the damn button now!"

Before Tobias could respond to her screaming instructions, the earth beneath them shook as a thundering beast emerged from the treeline. Two bright yellow eyes gleamed with sadistic joy.

"What the f—" Tobias said, frozen in place from fear.

Katana put a foot in her left stirrup and swung herself up onto Altair's back. She didn't even bother unhooking his reins; she knew she could direct him with the weight from her seat bones, not that he needed direction. His own natural instincts combined with his training would keep them both safe enough to do the required job.

The second Katana's bum hit the saddle, Altair took off. Half concentrating on finding her right stirrup and half concentrating on keeping a hold of her huge sword, Katana was completely at the mercy of her chestnut Arab gelding and to an extent, whatever God existed in this messed up world.

Seeing Katana race away from him, Tobias suddenly sprung back to life, but dropped his phablet in the process. He turned and bolted for his helicopter, shouting and waving his arms at the handful of men inside.

Three burly men, all dressed in black, jumped out of the side doors, huge machine guns positioned in front of their chests and all pointed at the raging werewolf. They let loose with their fire, a continuous, deafening noise filling the air as they emptied their magazines at the approaching beast.

The onslaught of bullets barely slowed the werewolf. When he saw Katana and Altair galloping off to his left, he changed his direction; fixed on his target of a female hunter.

Tobias' men re-loaded with more ammunition, emptying a second magazine each in the direction of the rabid creature.

Altair dashed into the trees, picking through narrow pathways and gaps in between their twisted trunks and branches. Katana had now gained her right stirrup and was fully balanced, poised on top of her steed with both hands wrapped around the tang of her lethal weapon.

A strangled bellow sounded behind them. The werewolf roared in frustration at the trees and branches blocking his path.

So consumed with the direct path in front of him, he'd failed to notice the gentle curve Altair had taken, leading back around to the left to exit the woodland where the beast had charged from.

Bursting out of the undergrowth with the speed of a bullet leaving a gun, Altair kept on his left-hand circle, intent on coming up behind the beast so Katana could swing her sword and end its life; albeit temporarily.

189

But the creature figured it out before they re-entered the forest behind him. He crashed back through the path he'd already cleared and leapt from his place, landing to the left-hand side of Katana and her horse.

Katana sucked in a deep breath and swung her sword through the air. The damn creature had landed half a foot too far away.

It howled with laughter.

Altair turned on the spot, as agile as a Spanish horse in the bull ring. Katana lifted her arms above her head and readied herself for another swing from the other side. Just as she lifted her blade, ready to swipe at its head, the monstrous thing exploded, showering her and Altair in blood and guts.

Altair halted, allowing Katana to wipe her eyes clean, re-sheath her sword, and then clean the chunks of flesh and bone from her face and body.

She nudged Altair forwards, turning him in Tobias's direction. When she saw her fiancé, grinning from ear to ear and waving his phone through the air, Katana couldn't help but smile.

"That went with more of a bang than I thought," he yelled, jogging towards them. "I like this button. Fancy a fireworks show tonight?"

Katana laughed. "I hate to ruin your joy, but he will be back."

"What?" He motioned his hands over her and Altair. "Have you forgotten the fact you're wearing him?"

"Oh no, not at all. But what you failed to recognise is that he's a phoenix hybrid. All you've done is killed him for half an hour, tops."

Tobias's eyes widened. "This really is a can of worms isn't it?"

"You have no idea."

31

"Husband," said Shania Kempe. Her cool tone told him in no uncertain terms he was bothering her.

"Hey sweetheart," Malaceia said, trying to soften her as much as possible. "I may have a little situation here I need your help with."

Shania glanced at her co-workers and mouthed her apologies as she stood from their round mahogany table and walked out of the small grey room. "This better be good."

"Well, I don't want to bore you with details, but I suspect Katana's friend, Erica, may have been meddling with Katana's profile on the system."

Shania rolled her dark eyes. She knew where this was going. Malaceia Kempe was far too predictable some days. That and he usually always failed to shield his mind. "And you want me to compromise her in her very first shield exam to see what she knows?"

Silence.

"You're too predictable, Malaceia. It's boring. Tell me why I should jeopardise my position in the coven, my relationship with my daughter, and my relationship with my fellow witches to satisfy one of your paranoid ponderings?"

"Because you're my wife and you love me?"

Shania snorted. "Strike one."

"Because you value our daughter's safety?"

"Why would Katana's safety be in question?"

"Because I suspect she's somewhere we don't know about. There are notes on her profile under Sophia's name—but Sophia didn't write it. You know how much of a geek Erica is when it comes to technology."

Shania rolled her eyes. "I'll think about it." She promptly ended the call and marched back into the meeting she'd been chairing. "I do apologise for that ladies. Please forgive me." Shania clapped her hands together and stood in front of her high-backed wooden chair. "Now. Are we ready to begin today's exams?"

ഇരുCരു

Erica was sweating more than a tennis player at high noon in the middle of summer. Passing her shield exam, the first official step to her being approved to work with the elite Kempe family, carried the utmost importance to her.

It wasn't just the fact she wanted her career as part of the elusive Amethyst Coven, but also that she knew things about the Kempe's inner workings that she really shouldn't know.

If she failed this exam, Shania Kempe, Malaceia's unforgiving Irish wife, would be privy to it all.

More than aware the Atwood name was at risk, especially after their previous indiscretions from two centuries ago, Erica was feeling the pressure from all sides regarding this 'baby step' exam. If she failed, she could re-take of course, but that wouldn't stop the secrets she knew from being out in the open to the scariest woman she knew.

Sat on a wooden bench outside the Amethyst Coven building, Erica prayed her exam would be over soon.

At that precise second, the glass double doors swung open and out walked Shania Kempe. Perfectly maintained with her glossy blonde hair and her natural looking make-up, Erica couldn't help but notice how much Katana looked like her mother.

Shania's skirt suit, white with black edging, really set a 'no messing with me' aura to her as she stood in front of her target and narrowed her eyes. "Are you ready, Miss Atwood?"

Erica looked up and nodded.

"Before we go in, perhaps I should extend the invitation to share anything with me I may find in your mind should you fail the exam."

Erica's mouth dropped wide open. Had she been caught already?

"So, do you have anything floating around in that head of yours that may concern me or my family?"

Erica faltered, not really knowing what to say. After all, what could she say?

32

After being showered in the body parts of the werewolf, Katana wanted nothing more than a nice warm shower—for her and Altair.

Tobias insisted they stop by the house that his family owned out here. "It's not far from here, we can easily walk. We tend to rent it out, but no-one has been in it for a couple of weeks. It's not booked again until the end of the month."

"Thanks," Katana said, leading Altair down the grassy hill. "How long have your family owned a property out here?"

"Quite a few generations actually." He cleared his throat. "I should probably now confess a little secret to you."

Katana raised an eyebrow and shot him a steely stare. "I really do think I'm done with secrets. Is it something I have to know?"

"Well…" Tobias bobbed his head from side to side "…if I don't tell you and you find out on your own, chances are you'll be more than pissed at me for not telling you. I don't see anyone else telling you either and I don't want to enter this marriage being dishonest from the get-go."

At the mention of marriage, Katana tried her best to ignore the scrunch in her stomach. The idea still didn't sit well with her, but she'd agreed the price already. Her debt was still to be paid.

She pondered over his statement for a few seconds and then nodded her head. "Ok. Thank you for wanting to be honest. It's much appreciated given the current circumstances."

"I hope the same courtesy would be extended back to me?"

"Of course."

He nodded his head. "Ok, so, you know that Jacques was born and raised around here, and also unfortunately kidnapped from around here."

Katana's heart skipped a beat. "Yes…"

"Well, he's technically part of the family. This house and land was given to his mum by my grandad."

"He's part of your family?" Katana stopped walking.

"Yes…his mother, Ava, is my father's sister…my aunt. He's technically my cousin."

Katana let this information spin around in her head for a few seconds. She couldn't believe it. Did Jacques know this? Was this why he was so against the idea of her marrying Tobias? "There's no technically, Tobias. He is your cousin."

He nodded and shrugged his shoulders. "Technically just kind of softens the blow."

"No," she said, shaking her head. "It really doesn't. How long have you known that?"

Tobias visibly winced. "Since he was taken. But I swear, I had no idea your father was involved or where he'd gone."

Katana narrowed her eyes and fixed her face with an impassive glare.

"My father and my aunt weren't particularly close. Nothing untoward, he just didn't approve of Hugo, her husband." He shrugged his shoulders. "Mainly because he was a shifter. Anyway—"

"Erm, you do realise that's being racist?"

Tobias stepped back, completely caught off guard by Katana's direct, sharp toned question. "I…there's a lot of politics with our family and the standing it has. Ava was supposed to marry into good standing not—"

"For love?"

Silence covered them both. Katana was growing increasingly agitated at the shady politics going on under everything in this world.

Why couldn't it just be a simple case of keeping human civilians safe from werewolves? Why did families linked to the Council have to marry other high-standing families? Why was there no love involved in anything?

"Love isn't the answer for everything," Tobias replied, keeping his voice quiet. "Sometimes it's more about keeping peace and allies. Especially in a world dominated by the supernatural."

Katana looked straight ahead, noticing a beautiful farmhouse in the distance. She started walking again and said, "Carry on."

"Yes, aunt Ava. When Jacques was kidnapped, it was the first I knew of her existence and of the existence of my cousins. It was only when I started training for the Council that I learned about your family using wolves to hunt and put two and two together. Jacques being a white wolf, that's very rare for shifters, you know."

Katana spared him a brief glance. "How so?"

Tobias shrugged his shoulders. "I don't know the genetics of it but it's kind of like albinism in any breed. It's rare and usually the result of a defective gene somewhere in the DNA."

"Maybe it came from his father's side?"

Tobias shook his head. "No. I've done my own research into it, more from curiosity than anything. Now, I'm no scientist, that's for sure, but I think the stress and trauma of Jacques' ordeal caused his albinism."

Katana's mouth dropped wide open. "What? Is that even possible?"

"Yes. DNA is an adaptable molecule. When something causes it to change, it's called a mutation."

Katana nodded. "Like the X-Men."

Tobias laughed. "Kind of. Depending on what molecule mutated depends on the change then reflected in the person. Studies at Harvard have been conducted on mice that proved that when exposed to chronic stress, their DNA physically altered. The reported mutations brought about changes mostly associated with mental illness or the autism spectrum. Of course, it's only mice, but imagine the catastrophic effects that can have on a human. Add in someone who is half shifter, with all the supernatural magick flowing through their veins, and you suddenly have genetic changes that no-one can predict."

"Wow," Katana said, all but breathless. This was astonishing news. "How else will it affect him if it managed to mutate his basic colouring?"

Tobias shrugged his shoulders. "It could affect him in any way. Mood, abilities, aggression, intelligence, fertility…"

Katana glared at him. "So if an environmental factor such as stress caused his genes to mutate, is it possible they can mutate back to normal?"

"Define normal."

"Well, how he was before the stress altered him."

"It's highly unlikely without fiddling with his DNA in a dish. It certainly could change, or mutate, again, but the chances of it changing back to how it was previously are very slim."

Katana sighed. "So it's likely he is how he is and that's it?"

Tobias nodded.

"What about altering something so he's able to shift again?"

"Now you're getting complicated. Imagine on the side of each cell you have two dimmer switches. One denotes the direction, i.e. forwards or backwards, and the other denotes the speed at which you travel in that direction. That's what will have been altered. Once you've altered one piece of DNA, you can use a virus to replicate its way through the rest of the body."

"Like with the werewolves," Katana said, a light bulb going off in her head. "Oh my God.

That's how we do it—how we save the people. We re-infect them with a virus that will kill off the original werewolf virus."

"I see your logic, Katana, but you're talking years of research, figuring out how Gregory got the virus to lock into the cells and replicate, then tests and trials…" he sighed and ran a hand through his hair "…half of the world will be dead by then."

Katana looked down at her clothes, still splattered with blood and pieces of flesh. "But me and Altair are covered in that werewolf's DNA."

"I don't follow."

"We're effectively wearing Gregory's work. There's a jump start right here." She grabbed a hold of her shirt and pulled at it excitedly. "The hardest part, getting his 'work' or whatever you want to call it, is right here."

"Do you realise what you're suggesting?"

"Yes," Katana replied. "I'm suggesting we save thousands of people from dying."

33

Jacques had a rough idea where to find Arald and Lenore. He'd heard whispers and rumours from other hunters and wolves over the years to know what was true and what wasn't.

He knew Arald was a civil, friendly version of Malaceia, and he also knew that Lenore was not quite the old scary hag most thought of when hearing her history.

After stowing himself away inside the back of a lorry, Jacques hitched a ride down to Devonshire.

In less than half a day, he was heading right along the Jurassic Coast to a small town called Salcombe Regis.

Situated on the edges of several tourist hotspots, Salcombe Regis was a small town that still thrived with its locals and the steady flow of holidaying families.

Out in the rural areas, Arald and Lenore were all but left to their own devices, known only to the locals as 'the odd couple' because they seldom took part in any community events.

Lenore wished for nothing more than to enjoy the fruits of life in peace and quiet. The less attention she drew, the better.

Arald, having had one too many fights with his hot-headed twin brother, wished for only the same, making the two ideal business partners.

Lenore, for all her magick trading for an immortal life had been worth, still carried a natural, almost 'human' like ability to sense certain things.

Psychic, for want of a better word. She could sense something big coming her way and she knew she had to help whoever knocked at her door.

Jacques obviously had a problem when it came to knocking on doors. Using his muzzle only resulted in a sore nose and a quietened, almost muted, 'thud.' Using his paws did nothing but scrape like nails down a blackboard.

When he approached the faded sky-blue door of the old farmhouse, he was pleasantly relieved, but not surprised, to see it already open, as if inviting him in.

All of the buildings in the local area were at least two centuries old, each harbouring its own quirky characteristics of days gone by.

This particular farmhouse was painted white, and where it would have once had a thatched roof, now sported a modern slate roof.

With its uneven, crumbling bricks on the exterior giving off a charming country vibe, the modern roof, all new and shiny, looked particularly peculiar and out of character for it. Almost like seeing one of your grandparents suddenly sporting lots of bling but still walking around with their zimmer frame.

Jacques placed a paw over the threshold and called out, "Hello?"

A woman appeared from a doorway to the left, around six feet inside. Her auburn hair hung in curls around her heart shaped face and her green eyes gleamed like freshly cut gems. Freckles dotted her nose and cheeks.

"Hello," she said, smiling. "I've been expecting someone. I had no idea it would be a wolf. Come on in."

Jacques padded inside, heading towards her. The delicious aroma of freshly baked bread trickled into his nose, making him sour for old memories once again.

Saliva pooled in his mouth as he remembered how good his mother's home-baked bread had been, especially when he slathered it in her freshly churned butter.

He entered the kitchen to see a huge room open out before him. Brick red porcelain tiles were under his paws, most of them dull and faded with age and wear and tear. A beautifully sculpted pine dining table sat in the middle of the room, four chairs either side and one at each end. An old aga kicked out heat to his left, warming a black kettle sat on top of one of the burning rings.

"Would you like something to drink?" Lenore asked, preparing two mugs with tea bags.

"Some water, please," Jacques replied. He'd not stopped for food or drink in his dire need to get here as quickly as possible.

Lenore looked down at him with soft eyes and smiled. "Now, you're not expecting to drink out of a bowl like a dog, are you?"

Jacques frowned. "Well how else do you expect me to drink?"

"I can give you a closed glass with a straw?"

Jacques found this rather curious. She was already treating him like he was a human before he'd even asked for her help. "Ok…I'll give it a try. Thank you."

Lenore nodded her head and reached to the cupboard above her. She pulled out a pint glass with a blue and white checked lid screwed over the top of it. A white straw poked through the middle. She unscrewed it, went to the fridge, grabbed a hold of a large jug with water and ice cubes in it, and poured it into his glass until it was full.

At just hearing the ice cubes clinking, Jacques found himself even more homesick. Memories of summer filled days running around with his siblings before heading inside to quench his thirst with some of his mum's delicious freshly squeezed fruit juice, complete with cool ice cubes.

"Thank you," he said, when Lenore set the glass down on the table and motioned for him to sit down.

Footsteps echoed on the wooden floorboards out in the hall. Jacques shivered when the rhythm and heaviness of them reminded him so much of Malaceia, and in some ways Gregory. Gregory weighed less than half of either of the brothers, so his footsteps never quite carried the thudding that Malaceia and Arald's did.

"Hello young fellow," came a booming male voice.

Jacques turned in his seat, somewhat nervous of the reception to expect from Arald. They'd not seen each other or spoken since Malaceia and Arald had had their big fight; just over six years ago.

"Hi," Jacques said. "I must apologise for the unscheduled visit. I really don't mean to barge in on you like this, but you know I wouldn't do it unless absolutely necessary."

Arald laughed and pulled out a chair opposite Jacques. He leaned across the table, his mass of weight making the old wood groan.

He and Malaceia were identical twins. Before their fight, the only thing that differentiated them was their belly buttons—Arald had an 'outy' whilst Malaceia had an 'inny.' Not a widely known fact to many.

Since their fight though, Arald bore a puckered scar that ran from the left side of his mouth all the way up his cheek to the tip of his left earlobe. Malaceia had his own scar that ran from the bottom of his right-hand ribs to his left hip bone. Arald had nearly eviscerated his own brother.

"No need for the babbling, Jacques. I knew you'd lighten my doorstep one day. How are things?"

Jacques shook his head. "Bad. I fear Malaceia and Gregory have gone into some sort of maniacal episode together. They've created a pack of over eighty hybrids. Gregory has let twelve of them loose, but that's not all. He's packed each of them with a virus—a virus that can change a human to a werewolf by a good old-fashioned bite."

Arald raised a dark bushy eyebrow. "We knew about the hybrids, but we didn't know about the virus."

Jacques frowned, trying to put things together. "You knew about the hybrids?"

"Of course we did," Arald replied, thanking Lenore when she presented him with his tea. "You didn't think it was slightly odd that one of Lenore's children was a test subject, but no-one had been to rescue him?"

"I hadn't actually given it much thought. There's been so much going on. So, did you volunteer Ashley or something?"

"Pretty much," Lenore said, sitting down next to Arald. "After the fight with Malaceia, we knew something needed to be done to stop things spiralling out of control. Obviously with Arald's involvement with the business up to that point, Gregory had been talking about experiments with hybrids and we needed a way to keep tabs on what was going on. We needed to know when it was time to pull the plug on The Red Riding Hoods."

Jacques gasped. "Pull the plug? As in make them go out of business?"

Arald nodded. "It's all well and good, having a few rogue beasts of the supernatural wreaking havoc here and there. It keeps things interesting and it reminds the humans that they're not as invincible as they think they are. However, the scales that Gregory and Malaceia are going to are something else entirely."

"Does Gregory know who Ashley is?" Jacques asked.

"No," Arald said, snorting. "The arrogant bastard was too delighted with his catch to bother with his background. To him, Ashley was a prize catch. He'd been through Cambridge Witch School and aced all of his classes—even coming out with a higher score than what his lecturer did when he passed. We made sure Ashley was 'vulnerable' and in the right place at the right time for Gregory to risk a kidnap. Worked like a charm." He took a sip of his tea. "Now, Gregory has unwittingly turned one of his own family into an immortal, murderous beast. What else can take down such a highly regarded family?"

Jacques eyes widened. Fear choked him. All he could think about was Katana. "But…but what about Katana?"

Lenore frowned and cocked her head to one side. "What about Katana?"

"Gregory sent Ashley after Katana. He told him they were soul-mates. He thinks that's his only 'in' to kill off the phoenix-hybrids—using their soul-mate as their weakness, but I don't know how…" something clicked into place in Jacques head "…dying of a broken heart. Oh my God. He wants Katana dead."

"What?" Lenore said, her hand trembling around the handle of her mug. "He sent Ashley to find Katana? Did he find her?"

"Yes. We've spent the past three days in Scotland with him. Katana's killed him twice already."

"No!" Lenore cried. "No, she mustn't. Each time she kills him, he loses a little bit more of his humanity. The werewolf will takeover eventually. If he dies enough, he'll never turn human again."

"But Gregory was killing him dozens of times a day in the lab?"

"Yes, but Gregory had a serum that stopped that effect taking a hold." Lenore looked down at the table and rested her forehead in her hands. "You must tell Katana to stop killing him."

"Doesn't Ashley know about the serum? He never mentioned anything to us?"

"No," Arald said, reaching out to Lenore and holding her hand. "We only know about it because we saw it on one of the spy-cams Ashley managed to set up down there. We've not checked in for over a week. We had no idea he'd let them go until Ashley called this morning to ask me about you. We've not spoken to Ashley in depth about it all since he went down there."

"Ashley thinks he's immortal, pretty much. He needs telling."

"When did you last see him?" Lenore asked.

"About ten hours ago. He lost control after Katana told him she'd agreed to marry Tobias Bembridge. He started to turn and yelled at us to get away, but he was turning at such a rate, we wouldn't have had much of a head start so Katana took his head off and gave us a good head start. As far as I know, he didn't chase the trail."

"Killing him will stop the werewolf transition," Lenore said. "But it just means that next time, he'll transition even quicker, meaning when he dies again, he's more werewolf than before. Eventually, when he rises from the flames, he'll rise a werewolf, not a human."

"I need to call Katana," Jacques said, looking around him for a phone.

"You said she's marrying Tobias Bembridge?" Arald asked, his intrigue more than spiked.

"Yes…she wanted help with the hybrids that are running loose and advice on what to do about her father and Gregory. Tobias named his price and she paid it."

"That's not a bad thing," Arald said, reaching over and patting one of Jacques paws. "There's no way Tobias would let Katana be prosecuted for any of this. She's unknowingly protected herself."

"All of this is Malaceia and Gregory anyway. What could she possibly be prosecuted for?"

"Guilty by association. Unwittingly taking part in what is essentially genocide without even questioning it."

Jacques sucked in a breath. "So what about her brothers?"

"They'll all go down," Arald said, shrugging his broad shoulders. "That's just the way it is. Even if Katana hadn't agreed to marry Tobias, she may have been looked upon favourably as she's the one to expose all of this."

"Oh my goodness," Jacques said, sighing. "This is so much more of a mess than what I anticipated."

"But Ashley and Katana aren't what you came to speak to us about today, is it?" Lenore asked, care and concern filtering through her eyes. "Ashley briefly rang me this morning to ask me about your…state so to speak."

Jacques nodded. "I wondered if there's any way to undo what Gregory has done. Surely there must be something that can help me shift again? Even if I end up stuck as a human for the rest of my life, I don't care. I just don't want to be like this anymore. I'm sick of it."

Lenore nodded and smiled. "I understand. We need access to you though to see exactly what Gregory has done. If it's more magick involved than science then I have a friend who can help. If it's more science than magick, then we may need some outside help."

"What do you need from me?"

"Your mind, my love," Lenore said, smiling.

Jacques balked. The idea of her reaching the deepest crevices of his tortured memories made him very uncomfortable. "Gregory is your son though," he said, pointing out the obvious. "Why are you not upset about his involvement and possible downfall in all of this?"

Lenore sighed. "To put it quite simply, Gregory should be in a grave, alongside his brothers and sisters who all died before the turn of the 1300's. When he decided to start dabbling in the occult and killing young children to extend his own life, he became dead to me. He's an abomination that needs stopping."

"But he's nearly as old as you. Why have you only just decided now to stop him?"

"I tried years ago when I first found out he'd gone into the occult. Up until that point, I understood that he'd managed to find a herbal drink to prolong his life. Of course, it was all just a big fat lie. By that point though, he was well and truly settled in The Red Riding Hood business and Malaceia was having none of it."

"But surely you turning people into werewolves was dabbling in the occult?"

"No," she said. "Not at all. That's simply using magick to alter their physical form based on a trigger—that trigger being the full moon. It's complex but is white magick. I've sought no help from demons to do that. Unlike Gregory."

"Gregory has been to demons?"

"Of course. What did you think I meant when I said occult? You don't gain access to black magick without a hefty price."

Dread tumbled around inside Jacques belly. "What kind of price?"

Lenore shrugged her shoulders. "Usually something cliché like the blood or soul of a virgin."

"Katana!" Jacques yelled. "Give me a phone. I need to call Katana."

34

Gregory had this all nicely mapped out. Everything had played out like a perfect movie. He would be set up for centuries to come whilst bringing in scores of cash for little effort; on his part anyway. The added bonus was he'd be cleaning the world along the way and doing everyone a favour.

He was currently sat in his lab, leaned back in his black leather chair, feet up on one of the work benches, with his hands pulled into a temple under his chin. He was waiting for a call from subject H7A2, Stefan Lear, to determine that he'd done his job successfully and killed Katana Kempe.

As a result of her death, subject number H5A2, Ashley Renata, would also die, if everything happened as it should in regards to his theory. Then the answer to his problem of having twelve test subjects that are unable to permanently perish would be found.

Also, along with Katana's death, his price to the demon Lazarus would be paid and Gregory would finally gain his status of immortality.

The people and souls he'd reaped so far were merely an 'offering' to show his commitment to living forever. Apparently, demons didn't take that kind of thing too lightly, purely because they had to share the earth with the immortal beings that they'd created.

Gregory rose from his chair and strolled through his lab. Heading for the back room, he opened the door that led to the 'dummy room,' skipped down the steps, crossed the cold tile floor, and opened the door on the other side of the small space.

When the heavy door opened into the underground room that so many people had been kept captive in, he grinned.

An eerie silence surrounded him for a few seconds before snarls, growls, and shouts of curse words filled the air.

He ambled over to the far side of the dank room, his shoulders squared back, and his head held high. In here, he was God. He could control whether these beings lived or died. He could control whether they ate and drank and even to what amount. Why they weren't worshipping him was still a mystery to him.

Walking down the long line of cages housing his experiments, he debated which hybrid to let loose next. The vampire hybrids had a particular thirst for blood he'd never yet seen in any werewolf. They would provide a good show.

The shifters were a bit of a disappointment. He'd gone too generic, he understood that now.

Initially, he'd thought using shifter DNA as a base would make the werewolf transformation quicker and therefore more aggressive. He was right; it did make the turn quicker, but it provided no additional benefit otherwise. They were just regular werewolves after that so a bit of a disappointment.

He stopped outside the cage of a young man who'd been the test for a werewolf-elf hybrid.

Elves were an unusually cruel species, excellent marksmen, and highly intelligent. When these hybrids turned, they were more of a lithe, athletic werewolf rather than a scary, bulky mass most commonly seen, but they had a trick none of the other hybrids had—they could pull their own teeth out with little pain and then throw them, like a dart, lodging them in their victim's necks. They could deliver the virus without ever being seen. These were a particular favourite of his experiments.

Maybe it was time for the next dozen to be released.

35

Erica, with the pressure put on her by Shania Kempe, crumbled. She couldn't afford to jeopardise her future in the Amethyst Coven.

Firmly believing honesty was the best policy, she confessed to the intimidating mother of her best friend that she'd been fiddling with their family business.

Shania took it rather well, which only put Erica further on edge. "Ok, tell me what you know."

Erica pointed at her temples and said, "See for yourself?"

Shania nodded and closed her eyes.

Imagining she was reaching out to Erica physically, she envisioned her fingers touching the young girl's temples and then pushing through her suntanned skin into her brain.

Shania was soon immersed in a 'disco' kind of setting with pulsating lights from Erica's over-active neurons all around her.

Memories were always kept at the back of the brain in a large pink box. Walking through the girl's mind, Shania soon found what she was looking for.

She opened the box and indulged in only the past three days of memories. She had no interest in anything else.

The memories were each contained in their own little 'book' so to speak. Shania merely had to pick each one up and flick through the 'pages' in order to see a fast-forwarded version of what Erica Atwood had been up to.

When she finished, only a couple of minutes later, she opened her eyes and studied the petrified girl before her.

"I see your intentions are honourable, Miss Atwood. I admire that, and I admire your honesty. However, with something as big as this, you should have sought higher authority to aid you in your tasks."

Erica's cheeks flushed pink. "I know and I'm really sorry, but I just wanted to help Katana. We didn't know how bad it was going to get."

"Have you spoken to anyone else about this?"

Erica shook her head.

"Excellent."

With that, Shania reached forwards and touched Erica's temples with both hands. She then surged dark vines of energy into the young witch's mind to erase any memories from the past three days that concerned the Kempe family.

Erica gasped. For the briefest of moments her face went blank as her mind rebooted itself back to current reality. "I'm totally ready for this exam, Mrs Kempe," Erica said, giving the older woman a beaming smile. "I know I can do this."

Shania grinned and stood up. "Perfect. Shall we go in?"

C.J. Laurence

36

The old farmhouse that Tobias's family owned was absolutely beautiful. Sandy bricks and a sprawling foundation across acres of green grass, it was quite an estate to own.

When Tobias had run into the old barn flanking the left-hand side of the house and brought out a hosepipe, Katana had never been so grateful to see running water.

Dowsing herself and Altair in cool, clear water, Katana scrubbed them both as best as she could. She knew she could thoroughly cleanse herself in the shower later, so Altair was her main priority.

When her phone kept ringing and ringing in her pocket, irritation only grew inside her when she wished whoever it was would just bugger off so she could clean werewolf blood and guts from her horse.

Her phone kicked in for around the twentieth time. She screamed in frustration and pulled it out of her pocket to see a number she didn't recognise calling her.

"Hello?"

"Katana, it's me, Jacques."

Relief swept through her. The fate of her friend had been lurking in the back of her mind since their fight earlier in the day. "Oh my goodness. Where are you? Are you ok?"

Jacques quietened her mind when he assured her he was fine. When he told her where he was, only more questions popped up.

"Why on earth are you with Lenore and uncle Arald? What's going on? Are you sure you're not in trouble?"

"No, I'm fine, honestly. Lenore and Arald are helping me." He went on to explain everything he'd since found out. "Gregory wants you dead, K. He made some deal with a demon."

Katana frowned. "Why does that mean he wants me dead?"

"Because the demon's payment is the blood or soul of a virgin."

"Oh." Katana froze, unsure what to do or what to say. "So what are you telling me? That I need to go and jump Tobias to save my soul?"

"Pretty much."

"Someone's changed their tune."

"Sometimes needs must. It doesn't mean I like it, Katana. It's a means to an end."

Katana felt a little hurt by his statement. She had no idea why, but it irked her. "Do you know he's your cousin?"

Silence fell for a few seconds. "I do, yes."

"When were you going to tell me that?"

"I didn't see it was relevant."

Katana snorted. "Right ok. So, is there anything else you know about that you felt I might not see as relevant?"

"Not that I can think of right now, no."

Katana let out a long breath, gathering her patience. "I presume you're staying with Lenore and uncle Arald for the time being?"

"It would make more sense, yes. I see little point in getting caught up playing a third wheel to you and Tobias."

"Jacques, please don't be mad at me. I had no choice—"

"There's always a choice. Anyway, if you need me at any point, you can reach me on this number."

"Whose—"

But it was too late. The line was already dead.

✄

Katana kept the latest developments to herself. She needed time to think over her options and assess any potential consequences that could arise from here on out.

After settling Altair in the old barn, Katana headed indoors for a hot shower. When she'd scrubbed herself almost raw, she finally climbed out, satisfied she had no more blood and guts on her anywhere. Her clothes were carefully bagged, ready to be taken to whoever Tobias may be lining up to help their cause.

Collapsing onto the king size bed that dominated the large, magnolia walled bedroom, Katana grabbed her phone from the small bedside table and dialled Erica's number.

"Hey chick," Erica said. "How goes it?"

"Not bad. You? How did your shield exam go?"

"Excellent. I passed with flying colours. Your mum even recommended me for a distinction I was so good."

"Erica, that's fantastic. I'm so pleased for you. We must celebrate when I get back."

"Get back from where? Bryn is taking me out this evening to celebrate. He told me to dress nice." An excited squeal followed Erica's sentence. "We're getting on so well, K."

"Scotland, Erica. I'm in Scotland remember?" Katana shook her head, curious at her friend's scattered memory. "That's brilliant news. I hope it carries on. Do you think it might turn serious?"

"Since when have you been in Scotland?" The shrill tone of Erica's voice would have cut through glass.

"Err...since three, nearly four days ago."

"And you're only just telling me now? Hell, I could have come with you and we could have had a little party."

"I'm working, Erica. What's wro—" A dawning moment hit Katana square in the face. Erica had been gotten to. That meant more than just her father being involved in this. "You know what? I gotta go feed Altair and make something to eat. I'll catch up with you tomorrow, yeah? Have a good time tonight."

"Thanks, honey. Speak to you tomorrow."

Katana ended the call and resisted the urge to hurl her phone across the room.

God dammit. Now what?

221

Now her only contact back home had been compromised, Katana knew time was a fickle friend right now.

37

Tired and exhausted from the day's events, it was no surprise that Katana ended up falling asleep after her phone call to Erica.

When Tobias gently shook her awake, she jumped like a startled deer. Not only had darkness settled outside, but the fluffy white towel she'd wrapped around her after her shower still cocooned her.

"Steady," Tobias said, chuckling. "It's only me, no big panic."

"It's dark," Katana replied, blinking the sleep from her eyes. "What time is it?"

"Close to ten p.m. I hate to wake you, but I have a couple of developments to inform you of."

Katana yawned and sat up. "Go on then, do your worst."

"The werewolf that came after us is definitely dead. I did a bit of digging into the exact structure of the council's microchips. When the detonate button is pressed, it emits a hyper EMP charge that effectively paralyses the supernatural cells. For a phoenix to rise from the flames, the supernatural cells have to be active and free."

Katana's eyes widened. "So he's really gone? You figured out a way to kill the immortal hybrids?"

Tobias shrugged his shoulders. "Well, not really. The answer was there all along. I just helped test it out."

Katana giggled. "Ok, well that's good—that we have a way to kill them. Is that everything?"

"No…my contacts, the people who could have helped us re-release a 'correction' virus so to speak, have assured me that the absolute earliest they could have anything ready by is two years. It's just not viable, Katana. I'm sorry."

A heavy anchor of guilt weighed down Katana's heart. "So what happens next?"

"I'm going to take you to the Council where you can explain everything in detail to them. Once you've done that, they'll conduct their own investigation, arrest your father, and deal with him accordingly."

At the mention of her father being arrested, Katana's heart twisted with pain. "And what about Gregory?"

"Gregory…yes, Gregory. He will also be dealt with but not by the Council."

Katana frowned. "Then by who?"

"A rather temperamental demon by the name of Lazarus."

Katana gasped. "How did you…know about him?"

"I had a phone call from my dear cousin whilst you were sleeping. He explained the situation to me."

Katana rolled her eyes and groaned.

"Don't worry," he said, smiling. "I'm not going to force you to sleep with me to save your soul or anything. I think we can protect you without us having to sleep together."

Annoyance began to rise inside Katana. Was he saying he didn't want to sleep with her? Why did this bother her so much? "Yes, God forbid you have to touch me."

Tobias eyed her with suspicion. "Are you angry at me?"

"Nope."

"You are, aren't you? You're angry at me because I've said I'd rather not protect you in that way. Do I get any points here for being a gentleman?"

Katana snorted. "It was just the way you said it, that's all. Like it was a God awful chore to have to even think about it. Am I really that bad?"

"You are kidding me, right? Have you forgotten that I've been waiting to marry you since you were a teenager? I'm four years older than you don't forget. That's a long time for an angel to wait, let alone an impatient man like me."

A small smile passed over her lips. "You do know I can be a real bitch?"

He laughed. "Is this not being a bitch?"

"God, no. This is just being awkward."

"Then I have lots to look forward to." He reached over and picked up one of her hands. Slowly, and waiting for her to reject his move, he watched her as he brushed a kiss over the back of her right hand. "You are an amazing woman and I can only thank my lucky stars that your father supported our proposed union. Any man would be honoured to have you."

"So when are we going to the Council?"

"First thing in the morning."

Katana nodded. A red blush started to creep up her cheeks. She patted the empty space next to her and said, "That means we have all night then."

Tobias balked at her brash statement. "Are you insinuating what I think you are?"

Heat raging through her body, Katana peeled her towel off and nodded. "It's going to happen at some point, right? May as well be for a good cause."

Tobias laughed before taking them both beneath the covers.

38

The next morning, a little sore and aching, Katana found herself being taken to Norfolk in Tobias's helicopter.

Altair had remained at the farm estate under firm reassurance from Tobias that once everything with the Council had been dealt with, they would return there for a brief reprieve. The farmhands who tended to the other livestock on site would tend to Altair alongside their normal duties.

As the hours ticked by, nausea and nerves tumbled together in Katana's stomach as endless possibilities raced through her mind.

The plan was for Katana to go home and confront her father, give him the opportunity to correct his wrong-doings, and if he didn't accept, then Katana would approach the Council.

Confronting her father had never been an issue for Katana before. Saying what she thought and asking questions was just a part of who she was, but this time was different. This time would only result in catastrophic consequences one way or another.

For the time being, the eleven phoenix hybrids were running around, wreaking havoc and flooding the Kempe business system with new cases hourly.

Whilst Tobias had the power to 'end' them all, Katana still needed to see if her father possessed any redeeming qualities.

Katana had already stated that she wanted, and needed, Tobias by her side. Her father could certainly keep her prisoner inside the house, but he definitely couldn't keep a Councillor's son hostage without further consequence.

The slow realisation of how correctly arranged marriages could work was starting to dawn on Katana but she kept her musings to herself.

Just before lunchtime, Tobias's helicopter landed back at his family home in their large twenty-acre field. A herd of alpacas stood under a copse of trees in the distance, watching with intrigue as the black aircraft settled on the neatly trimmed grass outside the large mansion.

"You've got alpacas?" Katana asked, squinting her eyes in their direction.

"Yes," Tobias replied, smiling. "Why do you sound so surprised?"

Katana giggled. "I don't know. I guess I expected big scary dogs or a golf course or something, not a herd of cute furries."

A haughty laugh left Tobias as he walked them towards the waiting black Mercedes on his gravel driveway. "Is that really the kind of image I portray?"

"Pretentious? Totally."

Chuckling to himself, Tobias opened the passenger door for Katana. When she settled in the black leather seat, he closed the door before getting in the driver's side. "I guess you're going to say you were expecting a chauffeur driven limo, too?"

Katana's cheeks flushed pink. "Well, you know what they say—like father, like son."

"Definitely not applicable here."

The pair fell into silence as Tobias started the car and headed down his long, winding driveway.

As the landscaped grounds slipped by, with trees dotted in random places, Katana allowed her mind to wander with fantasies of her and Altair ambling around the extensive grounds on a hot summer's day, just relaxing and enjoying each other's company instead of chasing werewolves and pools of blood.

Maybe, just maybe, the hunter life could be bypassed for a life of chilled out peace and relaxation.

The thought of the arranged marriage still made her feel uneasy, but she reminded herself that she'd agreed to the price and she had to honour the payment.

Her and Tobias seemed to get along well but how would this be in five years, ten years time? Would they be nothing more than hostile business partners like her parents?

She pushed the thoughts away, not wanting to think on the inevitable just yet.

Half an hour later, Katana's own family estate came into view. Tucked deep into the English countryside on the edges of Sherwood forest, it was the perfect place for any up and coming hunter to train with little outside disturbance.

Her family home wasn't as large as Tobias's but was still a good size to house the husband and wife and their seven children; each with their own bedroom. The large grounds were more than adequate to serve as training grounds for basic fitness, learning to ride, and of course live battle with real werewolves.

A supernatural electric fence bordered the perimeter of the Kempe grounds. The witches from the Amethyst Coven had created a spell that was uniquely keyed in to the werewolf supernatural cells.

If any werewolf attempted to cross the boundaries, they would be zapped with a force equivalent to 10,000 bolts. It would render them unconscious for hours, ensure outside civilian safety, and teach the brutes a lesson too.

Katana hadn't quite decided yet how to approach the subject with her father. After last night's phone call with Erica, she had a few choice words for her mother too. The thought of having to deal with six angry brothers hadn't even crossed her mind yet.

As Tobias pulled up outside the brick red house, Malaceia opened the front door, his face fixed in a look of thunder. When he noticed Tobias and Katana getting out of the brand-new Mercedes, he literally rocked back on his heels.

"Fancy seeing you two together," he said, his dark eyes lighting up with joy. "I was just on my way out, but I can tend to that later. Come on in." He held the door open and motioned them both inside. When Katana passed him, he frowned and said, "No Jacques?"

Katana fixed him a cool glare and said, "No. We need to talk."

Malaceia's smile started to fall. He looked at Tobias, as if hoping for some sort of clue as to what was going on. When all he received back was a blank stare, he pointed towards his office. "My office, then?"

Tobias placed a hand on Katana's lower back and directed her towards her father's office. Katana was obviously more than aware of where her dad's office was, but the small gesture carried a heavy passive aggressive meaning that the two of them were joint in their venture here today.

When Malaceia noticed it, he pursed his lips and swallowed the lump in his throat.

As the two walked into his large office, he closed the door behind him as he followed them. They both sat down in the coffee coloured seats in front of his desk, leaving Malaceia with little doubt that today's visit was formal.

"So, is this good news that you're both together?" Malaceia asked, sitting behind his desk and clasping his hands together in front of him.

Katana squared her shoulders and shot her father a glare that could have curdled milk. "Cut the crap, Dad. I know everything."

Malaceia gave a nervous laugh and darted his eyes back and forth between his daughter and Tobias. "What do you mean 'you know everything'?"

"I know about the hybrids and the sick little experiments you've been doing. I know that Jacques is actually a shifter trapped in his animal body, not a wolf that was suddenly given the power of speech. I also know that you sent Ashley after me to test out a stupid theory on how to kill the phoenix hybrids which would have ultimately cost me my life. I know about the virus you're trying to spread, too."

Malaceia licked his lips and laughed. "My dear Katana. You do have a vivid imagination. Where on earth have you gotten—"

"Mr Kempe," Tobias said, leaning forwards in his chair. "With all due respect, we both know the extent of your underhand activities that you've been using The Red Riding Hoods as a cover for. What you should be doing right now is thanking your daughter for coming to me instead of going straight to my father and the Council. I think we both know that you wouldn't be given an opportunity to right your wrongs if my father was involved."

Malaceia fell silent. He dropped his eye contact and stared at his hands for a few seconds. "Is that what this is?" He looked up and stared at Tobias. "An opportunity to right my wrongs?"

"It is. This is your chance to press the kill switch on those microchips, kill all the mash-ups you created down there in that lab, and it'll never go any further. No one else needs to know."

"And if I don't?"

"Then Katana and I will walk out of here, go straight to the Council, and present them with our evidence."

Malaceia leaned back in his chair and chuckled. "And what evidence would that be exactly?"

"Perhaps the remnants of subject number H7A2, known as Stefan Lear. The camera footage from my helicopter shows the subject attacking myself, my men, and Katana before being blown up by my doing. The microchip, of course, is registered to you, Mr Kempe."

"That proves nothing. Those microchips could have been stolen from my lab."

"Was that reported to the Council?"

Malaceia narrowed his eyes and shot forwards. "Don't play games with me, boy. It will not end well for you."

Tobias stood up and stepped to the edge of Malaceia's desk. He placed both of his palms down on the edge of it and leaned into Malaceia's face. "Oh, believe me, this is no game, Malaceia. You have your choice—end it now and keep your business or we'll end you."

"And you're really going to do that to my daughter, are you? End her family?"

Katana stood up, rage firing up inside her. "You ended our family, Dad, no one else. I've agreed to marry Tobias, so my family is now his. I'll no longer have to carry your name and be utterly ashamed of where I came from. You're despicable."

Malaceia looked at his daughter and faltered for the briefest of moments. "Don't you understand this was all to secure a future for you and your brothers? Why don't you see that?"

"Oh I do, Dad, I do get the twisted logic of it. What you're failing to see is that when everyone is dead or infected with the virus, then what? Who's left to pay us the money if everyone we come across is a potential enemy?"

"Well, it's not quite like that. There are specifics that the virus will only key in to. We've ensured that the people who matter will remain people."

Katana snorted. "Have you even heard yourself? What the hell is wrong with you? How can you sleep at night knowing you've killed thousands of people?"

"Survival of the fittest, Katana," he said, shrugging his shoulders. "It's as simple as that."

"Is that your answer?"

Malaceia merely stared at her, impassive, blank.

"Fine," she said, grabbing a hold of Tobias's hand and turning to leave. "Survive this."

39

The Preternatural Council didn't have a building of their own. To do so would attract too many thoughts of attacks and other unwanted behaviour.

Instead, they acted in various rooms underneath historic buildings throughout England. Only the Council members themselves knew where they would be meeting and when, for each monthly meeting was held somewhere different.

Last month for instance, their meeting had taken place in the vast expanse underneath Rievaulx Abbey in North Yorkshire.

People seemed to forget that in the days gone by, especially where it concerned monks and any member of the Knights Templar, subterranean cities were their life; both in hiding things from the general public and as a means of escape. Everything had been so well built back then, most underground rooms and chambers were still accessible and usable now—if you knew where to go and how to get to them.

If a trial was needed for some reason or another, then only one building was used—Nottingham Castle. This was their main 'court' as it dated back to the age and was situated in the very heart of where werewolves were first 'discovered.'

If any of the elite families needed to call upon the Council whilst in England, it was done so by heading down into the dark underbelly of Nottingham Castle and lighting the seven torches that were positioned around the room; one torch for each Council member.

The Master and Mistress of the Amethyst Coven had created a spell that would act like an emergency call to each Council member, but only once all seven flames were ignited.

Above each torch, on the stone ceiling, was a 'hot spot' that would glow red once the flame beneath it had been lighted. It would then diagonally reach across the ceiling to its nearest neighbouring 'hot spot.' Once all seven flames were lit up, the zig zag of lines created a seven-pointed star. The instant the star was finished and alight, the seven-pointed star tattoo on each Council members wrist would warm and glow orange, alerting them to the fact they were being called upon.

To enable immediate attendance, each Council member had a small mobile phone, purely for Council use. When they dialled the number 777, they were immediately transported to the 'courtroom.'

Councillor Bembridge was the first to make his call. Tall and slim, it was clear to see that Tobias's physique had been gained from hours in the gym instead of being inherited.

With grey hair, a pointed nose and thin lips, Councillor Bembridge definitely wasn't as easy on the eye as his son.

"Tobias," he said, trying to hide the surprise in his voice. "And Katana. How lovely to see you both together. Was there not something that could have been said outside of the Council?"

"No," Katana replied, stepping forwards into the middle of the room. "I'm afraid I have some startling news that quite frankly, only the Council can sort."

Councillor Bembridge nodded his head but remained silent as he waited for the rest of his colleagues to fill their seats.

Katana looked at the dark wooden table curving around her and Tobias in a half-moon shape. Behind the table were seven ornately decorated mahogany chairs. Their high backs and intricate carvings gave them a certain feel of imposing that only a Judge could carry off.

Within two minutes, all seven Council members were seated in their chairs and looking at Katana for explanation.

The Council guards were the next to appear, their own tattoos and mobile phones alerting them and giving them access to attend court.

Fourteen men resembled ghastly ghouls, dressed in long black hooded capes and carrying a silver spear, commonly known as 'persuasion sticks.' The men positioned themselves behind the Councillors, awaiting their orders.

Katana took a deep breath. She looked down at herself, dressed in her official Red Riding Hood outfit and smoothed her clothes down.

"Councillors, thank you for attending court today. I'm sorry to call you but I fear the fate of the country if I don't seek immediate help."

Councillor Bembridge narrowed his eyes. "This sounds particularly ominous, Miss Kempe. Please inform us as quickly as you can so we may act accordingly."

Katana took a deep breath and started from the beginning.

ဆၣ

"Well, Miss Kempe, that is quite a story," said Councillor Mayweather. "Do you have any evidence to back up your claims?"

Tobias stepped forwards and laid a clear bag on the table. "Inside the bag are Katana's clothes containing the remains of subject H7A2. Any investigation into the DNA of the tissue will support Miss Kempe's claims. I also am willing to provide a witness testimony and also video evidence of the creature attacking myself and Miss Kempe just yesterday."

"Mr Bembridge," said Councillor Stokes, a stout red-faced man who suffered no fools. "I'm curious why you didn't approach your father outside of the Council about this matter first?"

"Because in my opinion there is no other action that can be taken." Tobias reached inside his jacket pocket and pulled out a small black object. He laid it on the table and pressed a button. Malaceia Kempe's voice boomed around the room.

Katana gasped when she realised it was the conversation they'd had with her father barely an hour ago. Of course, in it, he admitted his own guilt.

When the recording ended with Katana's voice of contempt saying, 'survive this,' Tobias switched the recording device off.

Seven pairs of eyes fell on Katana. "You do realise, Miss Kempe, that you are putting your entire family at risk?" Councillor Stokes said.

"Yes. I understand the depths of this but it's not something I could sit on and do nothing about. I believe my father needs to answer to someone and the only authority he can answer to is the Council."

"Very well," said Councillor Bembridge. "Based on the recording we've all just heard, we will issue a warrant for Malaceia Kempe's arrest immediately. Please take a seat at the back of the room whilst the matter is dealt with."

Tobias took hold of Katana's hand and led her to the shadows at the back of the vast room. Murmured voices of the Councillor's echoed around them but they were all too muffled to pick out exactly what was being said.

"You did good," Tobias said, squeezing her hand. "Now all we have to do is sit and wait."

40

The wooden chairs Katana and Tobias were sat on weren't particularly comfortable. By the time Katana's ass had gone numb though, her suffering was over.

A faint purple haze shimmered into existence in the shape of a doorway. Seconds later, Malaceia Kempe faded into view, flanked by two Council guards and the Master and Mistress of the Amethyst Coven.

"Malaceia Kempe," said Councillor Bembridge. "You have been brought here today accused of crimes so severe, you may never see the light of day again." A brief pause. "Miss Kempe?"

Tobias squeezed Katana's hand and walked into the middle of the room with her.

Katana looked around her, dumbfounded and lost with what to do next. This was it—the moment, do or die.

She had her entire family on one hand—a whole history of twisted secrets and lies that she'd known about for less than a week.

On the other hand she had morals; the basic principles of right and wrong, following the law and keeping innocent people safe and alive.

"Miss Kempe," Councillor Bembridge said. "I have to say we never expected such a turn of events. We all suspected of course, that something must be going on to warrant the increased number of werewolf attacks over the past few days, but we suspected some ill-playing humans to be at the bottom of it, not your own family."

A weak smile passed over her pale lips. What was she supposed to say to that?

She looked over at her father, bound in heavy chains and gagged with a leather strap. His big brown eyes, the same chocolate coloured eyes she'd adored and trusted so much since before she could remember, pleaded with her to forgive him.

But that was a tall order. How can you ever trust someone who built your entire life on shaky foundations at best? Everything Katana had ever heard or been taught was all just a fabrication in the complicated web of the Kempe family.

Councillor Mayweather cleared her throat, interrupting Katana's thoughts. "On the basis of time, and of course the beginning of officialities, this is your last chance, Miss Katana Kempe. Do you wish to hand your father over to the Preternatural Council to stand trial for the crimes for which your family has committed?"

Blood is thicker than water, Katana thought. *I can't do this. Despite everything, I can't hand my own father over to the Council, can I?*

"Miss Kempe?" Councillor Bembridge said, tapping his foot on the concrete floor.

Katana cleared her throat and glanced around the room. "I...umm..." She caught sight of Jacques in between two figures in the shadows, her faithful friend to the end, hanging his head in shame. What a sad tale he had to tell—all because of her father.

Closing her eyes and taking a deep breath, Katana opened her mouth and replied, "Yes. I wish for the crimes to be tried and for my father to be punished accordingly."

Muffled grunts came from Malaceia as he tried to get his daughter's attention. After a few seconds, Katana looked over at him and narrowed her eyes. "You had your chance. I warned you."

Seconds later, the door crashed open and in walked Katana's mother, Shania. Wearing her navy blue 'power' suit as she liked to call it, she strode to her husband's side and demanded to know what was going on.

"Mrs Kempe," said Councillor Reading, a very straight to the point Yorkshire woman who didn't believe in tact or diplomacy. "You are not invited to be in this room at this moment in time, unless of course you wish to plead your own guilt in the matters that your husband is being accused of."

"I do not," Shania said, snorting in disgust. "And my husband is not guilty either."

"I'm afraid, Mrs Kempe, we have evidence to contest otherwise. As you're aware, we work slightly different to our human counterparts and believe that someone is guilty until proven innocent. With the overwhelming evidence already collected before an investigation has even begun, it's safe to say that you and your family are currently suspended from any business activities. As we speak, guards are already seizing control of your home, assets, and all of that which belongs to the Kempe name."

Shania turned to Katana and all but spat at her. "You poisonous bitch. Are you happy now?"

"I will be when you give Erica her memory back."

A sharp gasp sounded through the underground room.

"Miss Kempe," said Councillor Bembridge. "Are you accusing your mother of using her magick to alter someone's state of mind?"

Katana grinned at her mother and turned back to the Council. "I am, yes. My good friend, Erica Atwood, helped me in the first few days by hacking my father's computer system and finding out about the increasing number of attacks. I stupidly involved her with developments from there on, unfortunately implicating her in the situation. Miss Atwood had a shield grading yesterday. When I spoke to her afterwards, she had no recollection of the events she'd helped with up to that point."

"Mrs Kempe," Councillor Mayweather said, her voice sharp and carrying a certain distaste to it. "How do you answer that please?"

"Not guilty of course."

"Mr and Mrs Ainsworth, Master and Mistress of the Amethyst Coven, would you care to carry out a Council ordered memory sieve please?"

Katana smirked.

Shania shrieked in surprise. "No, no, no. That's not necessary. I don't need anyone picking through my memories. I admit it, I'm guilty."

"Excellent," said Councillor Mayweather. "Guards—please cuff and gag Mrs Kempe also."

Four guards hurried over from the side of the room. In seconds, Shania Kempe was in the same state as her husband.

"Mr and Mrs Kempe, you are hereby placed in the custody of the Preternatural Council until a full investigation has been conducted and satisfactorily completed. At that point, you will be called to stand an official trial where all of the evidence gathered will be presented to you for you to make your comments upon. After that, you will be duly sentenced."

The guards started to move to take their prisoners away but were halted by Councillor Bembridge.

"The Red Riding Hoods is an organisation that must continue for the safety of the English people. I am, with the rest of the Councillor's blessings, placing Miss Katana Kempe, soon to be Mrs Katana Bembridge, in charge of The Red Riding Hoods with immediate effect. However, to prevent a repeat situation, I am also requesting Mrs Lenore Kempe and Mr Arald Kempe as acting CEO's alongside Miss Kempe."

A concurrent murmur sounded around the table.

"Excellent. Mr and Mrs Ainsworth, can you please devise a method of letting the rest of the

Kempe family know of the latest developments and to direct any questions to me personally." He stood from his chair. "That concludes todays court session. You are excused."

Katana watched, her heart breaking into pieces as her parents were led away. They would be kept at the Amethyst Coven building in the cells beneath its basement. Being in a building ran by and protected by witches was the safest place for them both to be.

"We have one problem," Katana said to Tobias.

Tobias nodded. "Gregory."

41

Gregory wasn't stupid by any means. However, when the pressure was on and the noose being tightened around his neck, he was careless.

As he scurried through his lab, sweeping all of his samples into his large black leather briefcase, he didn't expect someone to clear their throat behind him. He whirled around, almost tripping over his own feet as he did so.

"Mum?" he said, his voice almost a whisper. "What are you…doing here?"

Lenore stood a few feet away from her son and painted a small smile onto her face. "You didn't think you could let Malaceia take the fall for all of this, did you?"

Gregory opened his mouth, but no words came out. When Jacques padded up the stairs and appeared at Lenore's side, Gregory narrowed his eyes at the white wolf. "What are you doing here? I should have known you meddled somewhere in all of this."

Jacques calmly walked up to his torturer, and as the man backed up a couple of steps, lunged at him and clamped his powerful jaws around Gregory's genitals.

Gregory squealed and dropped his bag, sending vials of valuable samples rolling across the floor. "Let go, please. Ohmygod, please."

Jacques growled and bit down a little harder.

Lenore gave a genuine smile this time and folded her arms across her chest. "Do I have your attention now, Gregory?"

Gregory nodded.

"Excellent. See, I may have traded my magick for immortality, but I'm still gifted with some natural abilities. One of those is making alliances. Do you know who I made alliances with Gregory?"

Gregory shook his head.

"I believe you're quite familiar with him. He goes by the name of Lazarus."

Gregory's face paled to a shade of white never yet seen. "No, no, no, no, no, no. Please, tell me you're joking?"

"My dear child, when have I ever joked about something as serious as this?"

The staircase creaked and groaned underneath the floor. As the sounds filtered through the square hole next to Lenore's feet, Gregory started trembling.

A head of dark hair appeared, followed by the familiar face of Malaceia—except for a scar that extended across one cheek to the tip of his earlobe.

"Arald?" Gregory said, almost squeaking.

"You didn't think I'd miss this did you?"

"Before our dear friend, Lazarus arrives, there's something you can do," Lenore said.

"If it keeps him away, anything."

"Tell us how to fix the shifters."

247

Gregory took just a second too long to answer. Jacques bit down until his teeth scraped against each other.

The mad scientist screamed in agony. "Ok, ok, ok, ok. Just make him let go, please."

"Jacques?" Lenore said.

Jacques held on for a few more seconds then released his captive. He didn't back away.

Gregory pointed a shaking finger to a fridge in the far corner of the lab. "There's a tray of bottles on the top shelf. Red liquid. They're individually named."

"Named?" Jacques said. "Why are they named?"

Gregory swallowed the lump of fear lodged in his throat. "I took a sample of your DNA before I altered it. What's in the fridge is a virus. If you inject it, you're essentially re-injecting yourself with your original DNA."

Lenore narrowed her eyes. "Nothing is ever that simple and easy with you. What's the catch?"

"No catch. It's a simple flu-like virus that will override the one currently keeping them from turning back into a human. That's it, I swear."

"So I'll go back to being a normal shifter?" Jacques said, hope raising his voice.

"Yes," Gregory said. "Every one of you that is still alive and serving has their own bottle in that fridge."

Jacques narrowed his eyes and snapped at Gregory's genitals. "Why did you keep it—our original DNA?"

"Because with changing times there has to be changing methods. There's no telling when we'd need the original DNA again to work as a base from for something else. It may have even worked to have you back as shifters in the future, who knows?"

Arald marched over to the fridge and pulled out a tray of small clear bottles with red liquid filling half of each bottle. He set it on the work surface next to him and started looking for Jacques' bottle.

A cold chill blew through the open staircase and whistled around the lab. Gregory paled. He looked at Lenore. "Please, Mum. You can't hand me over to a demon. I'm your son."

"You stopped being my son when you started killing children for your own selfish demise. You have magick, Gregory. You could have simply traded it for immortality like I did."

"And what use is that?" he shouted. "What's the point in being immortal but with no powers? You're just the equivalent of a dumb human except you can't die."

"If you want something to better your life, it's only right that you sacrifice something from your life. That's how it works, Gregory."

"And how have you bettered your life by being powerless?"

"It's taught me patience, dear child, and now I have my reward."

Gregory frowned. "What reward?"

A blast of icy wind whipped around the room. The overhead lights flickered. A dark shadow skimmed over the far wall.

"What reward?" asked Gregory, his voice quivering in panic.

The room fell into darkness for several seconds. The temperature dropped to such a degree, each breath exhaled left a cloud of mist in the air.

When the lights blinked back into life, a dark shadow stood next to Lenore. Around six feet tall but lacking defining features, the demon was a fuzzy edged being. Two red glowing eyes settled on Gregory. A bright white line of teeth then showed as the demon smiled.

"Gregory Kempe," the demon said, his deep commanding voice booming around the large room. "You have failed to pay the price demanded for our deal. The soul you marked for me to claim is no longer of interest to me."

"Katana Kempe? But she's…she's what you wanted."

The demon rushed forwards, gliding over the smooth floor. "She was yes, until around fourteen hours ago."

A strangled cry left Gregory. "But I was so close…isn't there something else we can deal on?"

Lazarus grinned, the points of his teeth gleaming under the bright lab lights. "I'm afraid I have a new deal. One of much greater interest to me."

Gregory looked at Lenore. She stood behind the demon, grinning like the cat who'd got the cream. "What reward were you talking about?" he said to his mother.

"Your magick," she replied. "You know demons can't have souls with magick. It has to be the soul or the magick."

Gregory's eyes widened. "So you're going to have my magick?"

Lenore smiled. "Yes."

Lazarus reached for Gregory. Two thick dark lengths similarly shaped to arms grabbed a hold of the scientist's body. With no warning whatsoever, Lazarus plunged a roughly shaped hand into Gregory's chest. The crunch of his ribs being shattered reminded Jacques of twigs being stepped on. Blood spurted out from the man's chest.

"Come here," Lazarus said, looking at Lenore. "Give me your hand."

Lenore went to the dark shadow and held her hand out towards him. He touched her palm, and a few seconds later, a bright blue energy fizzled through the demon and into Lenore.

As the last of it trickled into her, the demon squeezed Gregory's heart until it exploded like a balloon. A pale-yellow wisp of energy floated through the air. Lazarus grabbed it, swallowed it, and then vanished in a black whirling circle.

Lights flickered again and the temperature in the room rose back to normal.

Jacques looked at Lenore, dumbfounded. "I never would have thought a demon looked like that."

She laughed. "They're dark energy, Jacques. There's so much of it, no physical form can contain it. As a result, they are just...that—a moving mass of black energy that can vaguely resemble an object."

"Does your magick work?" Arald asked, running over to her carrying a needle and a small bottle.

Lenore stretched her fingers out and pointed her hand at the wall. The entire brick mass exploded outwards, revealing a bright summers day outside. "I'd say so."

"Excellent. Now, let's give our friend here a quick injection and then see how things are going in court."

42

Using Lenore's freshly acquired magick, the demon-dealing trio stepped through a portal, arriving just outside the courtroom door.

Lenore opened the door, keeping one hand against the hinges to absorb the squeaks the aged metal usually groaned with.

Arald and Jacques stepped through into the underground room and skirted along the brick wall, in the shadows.

Quietly closing the door behind her, Lenore followed suit, a big smile covering her face when she heard Katana speaking to the Council. Never had she imagined this would happen.

Not long after their arrival, the court was adjourned, pending a full Council investigation.

The Council guards filed out above ground first, merging back into everyday civilians. Mr and Mrs Ainsworth created portals to transport themselves and their newly acquired prisoners back to the Coven's building. The Councillors were last to leave, along with Katana and Tobias.

As Katana and Tobias headed above ground, Arald, Lenore, and Jacques padded up the stone steps after them.

After being underground in the darkly lit room, emerging into bright summer sunshine made Katana's eyes hurt. Tobias handed her a pair of sunglasses as she turned to face her friend coming out of the small wooden doorway.

"Jacques, uncle Arald," she said, opening her arms. She bent down to hug Jacques first, then stood up to hug her uncle. "It's so good to see you again."

"You too," Arald replied. He stepped back and motioned towards Lenore. "This is Lenore."

Katana smiled and held her hand out. She was pleasantly surprised when Lenore ignored her hand and instead wrapped her up in a warm embrace. "It's nice to meet you at last. I've heard lots about you."

"Ditto," Katana said, giggling. "This is Tobias Bembridge—my fiancé." She glanced at Jacques as she said this, unsure of his reaction to her speaking those words.

Tobias and Lenore swapped pleasantries whilst Katana rounded on Jacques. "Are you ok? I've missed you."

Jacques nodded. "They took care of Gregory. And I have some news."

Katana frowned. "Ok. Do I dare ask?"

"Gregory kept my original DNA. He replicated it into a virus so if I ever needed to be turned back into a normal human shifter, I could."

Katana gasped. "So you're going to be a real human again?"

Jacques nodded. "I'm going to be a real boy."

At hearing his mimic of Pinocchio, Katana laughed. "Have you done whatever you needed to do?"

"It was a simple injection. Arald gave it to me before we left your house. I've just got to wait to get the flu and then I'm good."

"At least it's just a flu virus this time."

₨⌒

Jacques ended up in bed for five days when his flu virus hit. Whilst Lenore tended to him, Arald and Katana took some time to re-acquaint.

"I have to ask," Katana said, as they headed out around the Bembridge estate for a midday walk. "Is there anything going on with you and Lenore?"

Arald laughed. "No. Our relationship is strictly business. We both had the same aim. That's all."

"Good. It would be a bit icky otherwise."

Arald shrugged his shoulders. "Not really. With how watered down our bloodline has become through marriages, we're about as closely related to her as what we are to the Royal family. In fact, the Queen and her husband are more closely related than what we are to Lenore."

"I guess I'd not really thought about it like that. Marrying inside your family is normal for the Royals but frowned upon everywhere else. Strange social acceptance really."

Arald nodded. "There are a lot of strange things in the world, Katana. You've got a lot more to stumble across yet."

"I think I've had enough for now."

Their conversation was interrupted by Katana's phone ringing. When the caller display came up with Tobias's number, she answered it, smiling.

"Hey, what's up?"

"I just got news from my dad that the Council are releasing your house and assets today. You can go home at last."

"Oh, wow. Ok. That is good news. Thanks for letting me know."

Silence stretched between them for several seconds. "I'm not saying you have to go home," Tobias said. "I'm just saying the option is there if you want to."

Katana giggled. "I…it would be a little weird to be honest. Would it be ok if I stayed with you for a little longer?"

Tobias chuckled. "Considering we're going to be married at some point, it's more than ok."

Katana forced a smile. The idea of marrying Tobias still didn't feel right when the words were spoken. She figured he'd be someone she'd grow to love. In time. "Is there any chance Altair can come back? I'm guessing it's going to be a while before the trial and everything is over."

"Already beat you to it. He should be with you within the hour."

"You know me so well," Katana said. "Thank you."

"Wear something nice tonight. I'm taking you out for dinner. Be ready for seven p.m."

Katana grinned. "Ok. Where are we going?"

"It's a surprise."

43

Katana spent the rest of her day ironing out changes within The Red Riding Hood business with Lenore and Arald.

Jacques was in a deep sleep, according to Lenore, and wouldn't be needing her for several hours.

They decided the need for wolves to hunt alongside the hunters could be relaxed. Between the three of them, they all agreed that either trained dogs would replace the wolves or if shifters wanted to do the job, they could do so; and receive a wage like any normal job. They would, however, retain their right to shift between forms.

When the Council seized control of Katana's family home, they found Gregory's remaining hybrids in the lab. All of the microchips were detonated, ending the existence of eighty-three innocent people—including Ashley.

"Are you not upset?" Katana said to Lenore, wondering why the woman wasn't in floods of tears over the death of her adopted child.

Lenore gave a sly smile. "I can guarantee you that Ashley is not dead."

Katana frowned. "But we've seen for ourselves on the map where they all were when the button was pressed. His last location is up in Galloway Forest Park—where me and Jacques last saw him."

"Yes, that's where the chip is located."

Katana raised an eyebrow. "Are you saying he cut it out?"

"I'm saying I know my boy and I know he isn't dead. Call it a mother's intuition."

"But, Lenore, if he isn't dead then that puts us right back in the same spot as before. If the Council find out—"

"They're not going to find out. All they care about is the fact that the microchip has done its job and reported back that it detonated."

"Ok," Katana said, letting out a breath. "What if he wasn't the only one who took out his microchip?"

Arald cleared his throat. "Ashley only knew about his because we saw Gregory put it in the hybrids. If it hadn't been for that spy-cam, he'd be none the wiser."

"So none of the hybrids knew about the microchips in their bodies?"

Lenore shook her head. "Only Ashley."

"Are you not worried about him hurting people? He thinks he's immortal, Lenore. If he walks around like he's invincible, he's going to get hurt, die, and then eventually never rise as a human again."

Arald reached into his jacket pocket, pulled out a small bottle full of a red liquid, and pushed it across the table. "That is Ashley's original

DNA. Gregory had done the same thing for all the hybrids as he did for the shifters."

Katana gasped. She covered her mouth with her hand. "But then that means we could have saved all of those people? I'm guessing it just needed a quick injection, like Jacques?"

Arald reached over the table and covered his niece's hands with his own. "Katana, I know you feel responsible for those people, but you mustn't. Yes, we could have re-injected them, like Jacques, but could you have seen any of them keeping quiet about their ordeal down in that lab?"

"So they've been killed to be silenced—is that what you're telling me?"

"Sometimes a great sacrifice is needed for the greater good. This is one of those times, sweetheart. I'm sorry."

Hot tears welled up in Katana's eyes. "But I'm sure a spell or something could have been done to erase their memories—like my mum did with me and Erica?"

Lenore shook her head. "To erase that amount of memories would have been near catastrophic, Katana. It's one thing for a witch to be able to erase memories of a few hours here and there, it's easy to 'fill in' the gaps because there's not a lot to fill in. However, when you're talking about nearly two years worth of memories, that's impossible. There's nothing to replace it with. The people have all been reported missing or presumed dead by their families. It's a huge mine field to wade into and to do it with over eighty of them? It's too high risk for the supernatural world to be exposed. I'm sorry, Katana. This way was for the best."

"But some of them were supernaturals too—witches."

"Yes, we know," said Arald. "But the risk of them talking and leaking inside information back to their covens was again too great. The Red Riding Hoods have a reputation and an image to uphold. This world we live in is a cruel one but it's a basic premise that every supernatural being understands."

Katana sighed and nodded her head. "Ok, I get it. I'm not saying I agree with it, but I understand. They had to die to save the world. It's not a bad cause to die for I guess."

Lenore smiled. "It'll become easier to live with as you get older and learn more about this business, trust me."

Katana looked at the clock and sighed. "Our conference call with the Council is in two minutes. Are we ready?"

Right on cue, the old-fashioned looking phone in the middle of the table rang, making them all jump with its shrill tone.

Katana picked up the red-handled receiver, pressed 777 into the keypad and watched in awe as the phone transformed into a mini-projector screen.

All seven Councillors sat in the courtroom Katana had called them to five days previously. The guards were all stood behind them, an ominous omen to what was coming next.

"The Council have come to a decision," said Councillor Bembridge, chairing the call. "Upon reading Gregory Kempe's notes and diaries, we've come to agree with one of his perspectives regarding population control."

Arald and Lenore exchanged glances.

Katana gasped. "Population control? Is that his excuse for creating this virus? And you agree with it?"

"Miss Kempe, regardless of the fact we live in a world dominated by the supernatural, we still live within the modern confines of a human society. Anyone can see that housing, jobs, unwanted pregnancies, food shortages—it's all a direct result of the population growing too large for the economy we currently have to support it. All seven of us Councillors are in agreement that we have the power here to do something to help that problem."

Katana let out a long breath. "Ok. What are you suggesting?"

"Having spoken with Mr and Mrs Ainsworth, the Master and Mistress of the Amethyst Coven, they've agreed to aid us in our task. With immediate effect, the Amethyst Coven will now control the turn of all werewolves with magick. Science is strictly off limits, and magick for anyone without Amethyst Coven approval is also prohibited."

"Ok," said Arald. "But how are you going to regulate and decide who turns? There's nothing stopping the Ainsworth's from picking and choosing who they want dead."

"The Ainsworth's are currently producing an elixir. This elixir will be fed into the main's water supply, firstly around Nottingham, and then gradually introduced around the country, and then into mainland Europe. In particular, this elixir will target those humans who are weak to the emotion of lust."

"But you're just doing exactly what Gregory was aiming for," Lenore said, dumbfounded. "I don't understand?"

"Not at all, Mrs Kempe. From what we've uncovered so far of Gregory's work, Gregory had keyed the virus to take effect regardless of emotion. It was only the hybrids who were sensitive to the emotions. Anyone else would have been turned immediately from a simple bite. We're not doing that."

"So now you're going to turn people anyway but only if they're weak and give in to their lust?"

"Mrs Kempe, we're not sure exactly what you were expecting from us but keeping The Red Riding Hoods in business is something of great importance to the Council."

"At the cost of innocent lives! You're supposed to protect humans as well."

"And we are. We're protecting them from making themselves extinct. Did you know that the daily birth rate is twice that of the daily death rate? How do you propose the population is kept in check, Mrs Kempe?"

"Natural selection," Lenore said, snorting in disgust. "Not with supernatural help."

"So you're saying the organisation you originally founded over eight hundred years ago you now want shut down completely? Bear in mind here that the Council has let your indiscretions slide by."

"Excuse me?"

"Until this last week, we were under the impression that werewolves had been a natural animal, not that your magick had turned them all the way through the centuries. By all rights, Mrs Kempe, you should be attending your own trial, too."

"Are you threatening me?"

"No, Mrs Kempe. We're merely pointing out that we are willing to overlook your early transgressions and deceit in order to help things move forwards more positively. So, I shall ask you again. Are you saying you want this organisation that you founded shut down?"

Lenore pondered her answers for a moment. Maybe it was worth hearing them out. Not just to save her own ass from jail but to see what they had in mind. "No," she finally said. "I don't want it shut down. It's just a shock, that's all. I didn't expect the Council to back up Gregory's work."

"Mrs Kempe, let me reassure you that is not the case. The Department of Health relies on our werewolf numbers for nearly two percent of their mortality rates. That's a lot of deaths that suddenly won't happen if we shut The Red Riding Hoods down."

"Ok," said Katana. "So how will it work?"

"The elixir is keyed in to their deepest, darkest desires. We're going back to the basics of why the very first werewolf was ever created. I'm sure that's something you can get on board with, Mrs Kempe."

Lenore paled. "What are you saying?"

"Think serial killers, rapists, paedophiles—they are our targets. We're morally cleansing at the same time as controlling the population. It's not like they give in to the craving of a chocolate bar and suddenly turn—that would be Gregory's level."

Katana smiled. "The scum of society being turned into werewolves that we can then hunt and kill? I'm game."

Arald and Lenore laughed. Lenore sighed and nodded her head. "Ok, that sits well with us. When does this take place?"

"The elixir will start being fed into the water supply from tomorrow morning."

"Excellent news," Arald said. "Thank you, Councillor."

"One last thing before we end today's meeting. The trial was initially set to be next week, but we've brought it forwards to tomorrow. We're very aware of how much everyone wants this to be over. We have all of our evidence so there's no point in delaying it any longer."

Katana's heart dropped to her feet. A tremble of nerves took control of her body. She hadn't been to see her parents since they'd been taken into custody. She couldn't bring herself to admit that she was the cause of their current situation.

"Ok, thank you, Councillors," Arald said. "What time?"

"Ten a.m. Please wear your official uniforms." The call ended.

Katana, Arald, and Lenore looked at each other and shrugged their shoulders.

"Well, I guess we're still in business at least," Arald said.

44

Dressed in a classic black dress, Katana was ready for seven p.m. for her date with Tobias.

Nerves churned around in her stomach as the clock ticked the time away. Even though they were living in the same house, Tobias went to the extreme of walking out of his own front door and ringing the door bell as if picking Katana up for their date.

She answered the door, giggling. "Hello."

"Wow, you look amazing," he said, handing her a bouquet of red roses.

Katana looked him up and down in his own smart pale blue cotton shirt and black tailored trousers. "You look pretty nice yourself."

He smiled at her and made a hook with his arm as he motioned for her to join him outside. Walking her to the car, he settled her in the passenger seat before jumping in the driver's seat.

"Where are we going?" she asked, trying to ignore the grumble of her stomach.

"Well, you'll have to wait and see."

Katana gifted him a small smile before bringing him up to speed on the latest developments. "So it looks like we're going to be vigilante justice werewolf hunters."

Tobias chuckled. "That's a good thing, though. It's not just population control for the sake of it. It's gene cleansing, society protecting, and soul healing."

"Soul healing?"

"Well, yeah. You're telling me you won't enjoy going after some guy whose been forcing himself on little kiddies?"

Katana stilled for a moment, several thoughts running through her head. "Of course I would, it'll make the whole kill thing even sweeter. But I thought you weren't a fan of women hunting in the field?"

"Are you calling me sexist?"

"No…more old fashioned."

He laughed so heartily, a tear leaked from the corner of his left eye. "I like that. Very good."

"So you're saying that you'll be happy for your wife to go out hunting in the field?"

Tobias looked over at Katana and smiled. "We're nearly at the restaurant. I hope you like Thai food?"

Katana nodded. "Love it."

"Good."

They fell into silence as Tobias drove the last few miles. When he pulled up down a small empty country road, Katana frowned. He eased the car into a small gravel square, turned the engine off, and hopped out.

Helping Katana from the passenger seat, he eased her along the gravel as her high heels made her footing unsteady. Once over the gravel, they stood on a grassy bank looking into a narrow canal.

"Food awaits," he said, motioning to his right.

Katana looked to where his attention was focused and gasped.

A narrowboat sat on top of the dark waters, warm yellow lighting gleaming out of the windows and the delicious aroma of cooking food wafting through the air towards her.

"Really? That's a restaurant?"

Tobias grinned. "Ok. It's my personal boat that I hired a chef to cook in, but it still counts, right?"

Katana laughed. "Full marks for effort, definitely."

Tobias helped her cross the soft grass and step down the soft bank. When they finally set foot on the boat, Katana let out a long breath she didn't realise she'd been holding.

"Did that make you nervous?" Tobias asked, opening the small wooden door that led into the cabin.

"I invite you to put six-inch heels on and walk down a virtually vertical bank without holding your breath."

"I'll take your word for it," he replied, chuckling. "Wearing women's shoes isn't really my thing."

Katana giggled and stepped inside the narrow boat. Perfectly polished wood shone back at her. At the far end, a white marble kitchen stole the attention complete with a busy chef frying something in a wok.

A cream leather couch dominated the left-hand side of the boat with a long table stretched out in front of it. The table was set for two places with two tall candles lit and flickering with romance.

"This is amazing," Katana said, turning to Tobias. The sizzling coming from the wok almost drowned out her words. "I can't believe you've set this up. Thank you."

Tobias held his hand out towards the sofa. "The pleasure is all mine. I hope you're ok with eating on a sofa? I didn't have enough time to get it replaced with chairs."

Katana frowned. "What do you mean?"

"Well I had a team come in and spruce the place up a little. They couldn't get me proper chairs to replace the sofa ordered in time for tonight."

"How long have you been planning this?"

"Five days."

Katana gasped. The penny dropped as to what all the fuss was about. Her stomach tumbled and flipped around inside her. He was going to propose. This was it. The moment.

"Sit down. I'll get us some wine."

Katana sat on the smooth leather surface, trying to ignore the cold sweat that had broken out all over her body.

She watched Tobias as he strode towards the small kitchen, chatted with the chef, and then came back with an expensive looking bottle of champagne.

He popped the cork easily, poured two glasses, and then sat down next to her.

"So, you've probably guessed what tonight is for," Tobias said, taking a sip of his drink.

Katana nodded, a hot flush creeping up her cheeks. She took a gulp of her champagne to escape the rising tension.

"But, it's not going to happen," he said, giving her a sad smile.

Katana's heart stopped and did a back flip. "What?"

"I've been doing some thinking over the past few days and I have to agree with you."

"With me? On what?"

"Marrying for love."

A spear of dread lodged itself in her heart. She was being dumped by the guy who'd pursued her for six years? What the hell?

"But…our deal…I'm confused."

A thud sounded from outside. Tobias looked towards the door and nodded. "I know I'll never have your heart, Katana. After everything that's happened, I've come to realise that allowing you to be with the one person you love more than anything is the least I can do. You don't have a price to pay to me."

The door squeaked open. Katana looked in its direction. A tall, white-haired man stepped inside. His lithe, athletic body was highlighted perfectly in a white cotton shirt and a pair of dark denim jeans. Two sparkling blue eyes settled on Katana.

"Jacques?" she said, tears springing to her eyes.

"Hey," he replied, his pink lips turning upwards into a warm smile. A rosy blush spread over his face. "You look fantastic."

Katana bolted from her seat and rushed to her best friend, desperate to hug him for real. When he wrapped his arms around her and nuzzled into her hair, she couldn't help but let the tears slide free.

45

Tobias left Katana and Jacques alone shortly after Jacques' arrival. He had his own love he needed to find and pursue. When Katana's eyes had lit up with such joy at seeing Jacques and meeting him as a human for the first time, Tobias knew he'd done the right thing. He wanted to have someone look at him like that and he wanted to look at someone like that too.

∞⊗

Katana and Jacques cleared three bottles of wine and emptied the boat of food. A little after midnight, they teetered back through the front door of Tobias' house. He'd sent a driver to pick them up when Katana called for a ride home.

When she collapsed on her bed, fully clothed, her eyes were already shut before she could even undress.

All too soon, it was morning.

"Hey," Jacques said, knocking on her bedroom door. "Are you up?"

Katana groaned and opened her eyes. "Is it really morning already?"

"Unfortunately."

"My head is pounding. I think I drank too much."

Jacques laughed. "That's why I brought gifts." He waved a box of paracetamol at her and held out a glass of orange juice.

"Thank you so much," she said, reaching for them eagerly. She took two tablets and downed the juice. "What time is it?"

"Nine."

She gasped. "We've got to be in court in an hour. I haven't pressed my uniform either." She scrambled out of bed and grabbed a towel from the floor. "I need a shower too. I smell like stale alcohol."

"Don't panic. I've already sorted your uniform."

Katana looked at him and frowned. "For real?"

He nodded his head.

"You're the best," she said. She leaned over and kissed his cheek. "Thank you."

Jacques blushed. "No problem. It was my pleasure."

Dashing off to the shower, Katana couldn't wipe the grin from her face.

❧

Showered and dressed, Jacques, Katana, Lenore, Arald, and Tobias all piled into Tobias' Mercedes, ready to attend the trial of Mr & Mrs Kempe.

Sat in the back, Jacques and Katana were squished together as Arald dominated most of the space.

"How are you holding up? Being human again and all?" Katana said.

Jacques smiled, his eyes lighting up with happiness. "Loving it. I never thought food could taste so good. I had re-heated pizza for breakfast. Do you know how good that is?"

Katana laughed and shook her head. "Have you tried shifting back yet?"

A streak of sadness flashed through his eyes. "No. I don't want to. Not yet."

"Too scared you won't turn back?"

He nodded. "Sounds silly after everything we've been through, huh?"

"Not at all." Katana grabbed his hand. "It's great to finally meet you as a person, though. It's…different, in a good way."

He laughed. "I know what you mean. I err…" he scratched his head and looked down "…I need to apologise for my behaviour, when Ashley appeared. When I ran off. I'm sorry I was so dramatic."

"Hey, it's all in the past now. Done and dusted. Forgotten."

"Makes things a little awkward with us though, doesn't it?"

Katana giggled. "The awkward part is getting used to you like this. It's somehow easier to shout at a wolf and stay mad."

Jacques chuckled and grasped Katana's hands with his. "You know I meant it, though?"

"What?" she replied, licking her dry lips.

"That I felt you're supposed to be mine."

Water sprung to Katana's eyes and her heart started beating harder. "I know…I just…there's so much to adjust to right now. Heck, last night I thought I was going to be agreeing to Tobias' marriage proposal."

Jacques squeezed her hands. "I know. I'm glad he had a change of heart."

"Strange, really, but I'm not complaining. Still, I do have one thing to ask you."

"Go on."

"Well, I feel kinda dumb asking this, but I have to. My dad always said that if you were human you would be…you know…"

"In Vegas, wearing sparkly dresses and calling myself Jennifer?"

Katana laughed so hard, she cried. Nerves were perhaps a part of that too. "Yes," she said, between splutters of laughter.

"K, I hate to break it to you, but no. I'm not gay. I have no interest in the male species except on a platonic level. People like your father, the typical Neanderthal alpha-male types, don't tend to understand the men who are in touch with their emotions. That's all."

Katana pictured her father running around with a club, grunting, and chewing on raw meat. She laughed even harder. "He really is going to be Neanderthal-like when he's hauled up in court today."

Jacques gave her a thin smile. "I am so sorry this happened, K. Can you ever forgive me?"

276

"Forgive you for what?"

"For dragging you through all of this. After all, if I'd kept my mouth shut, none of this would have happened."

Katana wrapped her arms around her friend. "Yes, it would have. Maybe not this week, or this month, or even this year, but at some point, Gregory and my father would have come tumbling down from their pedestals." She smiled and touched Jacques' cheek. "You know what? I'm grateful that you trusted me to deal with it all. That says a lot."

Jacques curled his arms around her, holding her so close it was hard to tell where one started and the other ended. "That's exactly why I love you," he said.

Katana smiled and buried herself further inside his shirt, inhaling his intoxicating scent of fresh oranges. "I love you too."

46

The trial was no more of a public affair than when Katana had called them all to court previously.

When she walked into the courtroom and saw her mother and father stood before the Councillors, bound and gagged, it suddenly hit home harder than before about what was going on.

Jacques took her hand and guided her to the seats at the back of the room. The fact he was now human did not go unnoticed by Malaceia who watched him with great interest as he walked past.

Tobias had driven them all there with a minute to spare. By the time they sat down, the gavel was dropped and court was in session.

"Guards, please remove the gags from Mr & Mrs Kempe," said Councillor Bembridge.

Two guards glided forwards and unbuckled the leather straps around Shania and Malaceia's mouths.

"Malaceia Kempe, you are to stand trial for the following crimes; fraud, endangering civilian lives, illegal experiments on civilian lives, and gross misconduct. The Council have evidence to support these claims. How do you plead?"

"Guilty."

A strange silence fell over the room. After a few seconds, the Councillor resumed his speech.

"If you are pleading guilty, Mr Kempe, then we can move straight to your sentencing. Do you wish to move forward or would you like to hear the evidence the Council has collected against you?"

"Just give me my damn sentence," he said, sighing.

"These sentences will run consecutively. For the conviction of fraud which includes money laundering, false advertising, and obtaining money by deception—ten years. For endangering civilian lives—three years. For illegal experiments on civilian lives—thirty years. For gross misconduct—five years. That is a total of forty-eight years to be served. You will not be eligible for parole as you are a deemed a severe risk to the safety of society."

Shania turned around and glared at Katana. Hatred oozed from every pore.

"Mrs Kempe," said Councillor Bembridge. "Do we have your interest?"

"Yes," she said, turning back around.

"Good. Mrs Kempe, you are being charged with fraud, endangering civilian lives, gross misconduct, and abuse of power. The Council has evidence to support these claims. How do you plead?"

Silence settled around the room. Seconds ticked by.

"Mrs Kempe."

Shania gave a dramatic sigh and said, "Fine. Guilty."

"Do you wish to hear the evidence or—"

"Just get on with it."

"Excellent. Your sentences will also run consecutively. For the conviction of fraud which includes money laundering, false advertising, and obtaining money by deception—ten years. For endangering civilian lives—three years. For gross misconduct—five years. For abuse of power—twenty years. That is a total of thirty-eight years. You will not be eligible for parole as you are a deemed a severe risk to the safety of society."

For several painful seconds, no one spoke or seemed to even dare breath. Katana sat on her chair, clutching Jacques' hand so tightly, she failed to realise she'd cut off his circulation.

"You will both serve your sentences in separate facilities. Communication between you is forbidden from this moment forwards. Mr Kempe, you are to serve your time in the laboratory at your family home. Measures have already been taken to secure it into an acceptable prison."

Katana gasped. "What?" she whispered, glancing over at Tobias.

"That's absurd," Malaceia said. "What the hell is this?"

"MR KEMPE, please refrain from shouting out in court. It is not tolerated. The Council's decision of where you will serve your sentence has been decided by the severity of your crimes. We see it as only fair that you spend a significant amount of time in the same place that you subjected innocent people to. Our decision is final and appeals are not permitted."

Jacques took his hand from Katana's and placed an arm around her shoulders. "Bittersweet irony at its best," he whispered.

Katana nodded.

"Mrs Kempe, you will serve your sentence in the human world. Mr and Mrs Ainsworth will drain your magick as soon as court is over and wipe your memories of the supernatural world. You will likely perish in a human life before your sentence is over."

Katana choked back a sob. Her mother hated humans more than lions hate hyenas. To have no magick filtering through her veins would mean she had no protection from illnesses or diseases. She would just be a regular human. At nearly fifty, her mother would be nudging ninety before her time was done.

Shania whirled around and glared at Katana. "You fucking bitch! Are you happy with this? You've ripped our family apart. Can you sleep tonight knowing you've torn this family to shreds?"

"MRS KEMPE."

"You know you were an accident, right?" Shania said, narrowing her eyes at her daughter. "An unplanned pregnancy that I never wanted to keep. That's right—I wanted to abort you. I told your father you were a wrong 'un—I could feel it even when you were in my womb. He saved your life and this is how you repay him?"

All of the emotions Katana had been feeling up to now welled up inside her, rising in a strong wave that could only be expelled in tears.

Jacques wrapped her up in his arms and rubbed her back, soothing her tears.

Lenore stood up and rushed over to Shania. "You should have been aborted, Shania. The Amethyst Coven can finally flourish now you're not on the board."

Shania opened her mouth to reply but was silenced by one of the Council guards putting her gag back in place.

Malaceia turned to face his daughter. With her head still buried in Jacques chest, he had little choice but to speak to the man cradling his daughter.

"Tell her I'm sorry and I don't blame her. She did what was right. That's the true strength of a Kempe."

Jacques nodded and turned his attention back to Katana.

Less than five minutes later, the two prisoners were parted and sent on their way to their new lives.

47

"Have you heard from any of your brothers?" Arald asked Katana. She shook her head. "Not a peep. I think after they heard they weren't being charged with being guilty by association, they've kept their heads down."

Arald let out a low whistle. "But still. You'd think at least one of them would have something to say."

"Maybe in time," Katana said. "It's only been a week. Everything is still very raw."

Now back at her family home, with her father kept prisoner downstairs, Katana had welcomed Arald and Lenore to stay in the house, and of course Jacques.

Erica had decided that maybe working for the Amethyst Coven with all the politics involved wasn't the best move for her. She was now studying to be a primary school teacher. Still in need of money in the meantime, Katana had given her a job as a cook and a maid at her home.

"Please don't think I'm trying to de-mean you, Erica," Katana said, when she offered her the job. "But I know you won't accept money just for the sake of it and I need help keeping this giant house clean and tidy."

Erica had thrown her arms around her best friend and laughed. "It's perfect. Thank you."

Now, as Katana, Lenore, and Arald sat around the round mahogany table in Malaceia's old office, Erica burst through the door carrying a tray of freshly cooked chocolate chip cookies.

"Erica," Arald said, shaking his head with a laugh. "You're going to make us really fat if you carry on with this."

"Would you like me to stop baking these daily for you?"

"No, thank you," Katana said, giving her friend a smile. "I'm used to my eleven o'clock treat now."

Erica grinned, slid the baking tray across the table and skipped back out to the kitchen.

"Right," Lenore said, tapping on her iPad. "Back to business. With your brothers off the grid for hunting, Katana, that means we're six hunters down. That's quite a lot. We've already seen fifty new cases this week thanks to the elixir."

Katana nodded her head and grinned. "It's fine. I got this. It's time for me to pave the way for the women."

Arald frowned. "What do you mean? Where are these women coming from?"

"Well, it turns out that all three of my female cousins were paid off to disappear from the family line. I've tracked them down and they're interested in training up."

"What cousins?" Arald said. "There was only me and your father, and your aunt Marion. She left no children."

"Oh, she did. Dad had them all adopted out to witch families."

"You're joking? I've got more nieces out there?"

Katana grinned. "Yes indeed."

Lenore smiled and reached across to Katana, taking her hands. "If there's one thing your wolf was wrong about, it's that you would end up alone."

Katana nodded and smiled. "I've never felt more part of a family than what I do now."

ACKNOWLEDGEMENTS

Well, the most important acknowledgements need to go to you—the reader. Without all of you guys, authors would simply be mental people with voices instructing them of words in their heads, so thank you for sticking with us. I hope you enjoyed this tale. Katana will be back very soon!

WHERE TO FIND C.J. LAURENCE

You can find me in the following places:
www.cjlauthor.com
www.facebook.com/CJLaurenceAuthor
www.facebook.com/groups/lollipoplounge
www.twitter.com/cjlauthor
www.instagram.com/cjlauthor
www.amazon.com/author/cjlaurence
https://www.bookbub.com/authors/c-j-laurence

I love hearing from my readers and will always reply to you!
You can also subscribe to my monthly newsletter through my website and be privy to top-secret news, exclusive giveaways, and new releases.

ALSO BY THIS AUTHOR:

Want & Need by Limitless Publishing
Cowboys & Horses
Retribution – Breaking Free Journey 1
Craving: Loyalty by Crave Publishing
Craving: One Night by Crave Publishing
Mirror by Enchanted Anthologies
Unleashing Demons
Craving: Forbidden by Crave Publishing
Unleashing Vampires

COMING SOON:

Forest of the Dark by Enchanted Anthologies
Unleashing Werewolves
Dirty Little Secrets
Malus Malum Venandi – The Grim Sisters 2

30062272R00171

Printed in Poland
by Amazon Fulfillment
Poland Sp. z o.o., Wrocław